Lana Guineay is a writer who lives by the sea in Adelaide. Her non-fiction has been published widely, and her award-winning fiction has appeared in *Going Down Swinging*, *Anthology of Australasian Stories*, and the 2019 Swinburne Microfiction award. Lana graduated from the University of South Australia with an honours degree in Creative Writing, and followed a career as a content and fashion editor for global brands before returning to her hometown, where she works as a freelancer. *Dark Wave* is her first book.

First published in Seizure by Brio Books in 2020

Brio Books

PO Box Q324, QVB Post Office,

NSW 1230, Australia

www.seizureonline.com
www.briobooks.com.au

Cataloguing-in-publication data is available from the National Library of Australia

978-1-922267-25-2 (print)

978-1-922267-26-9 (digital)

Internal design and typesetting © Brio Books 2020

Cover illustration and design by Sam Paine,
www.sampaine.com

Edited by Alice Grundy

DARK
WAVE
LANA GUINEAY

my heart breaks
like surf.

The Monkey's Mask
Dorothy Porter

1.

The legendary George Green glistened, calling 'Ayyyy looking goooood!' with joyous bite to all present — surfers, God — in the sea that contained everyone and everything that mattered, the sea that grabbed the coarse-sanded beach of Bronte in its dark opulence: how beautiful is Sydney at six ay-em on the first day of summer? The only business that mattered to him was the business of surfboards, slapped with feet, tanned bodies in neoprene, business of the inspired kind, the mystic business of the weird sisters of grace, charm and beauty, whose influence was everywhere over humans and waves on this glinting morning, the sun still clothed in night's clouds.

Looking up. Usually single-minded, thinking waves and only waves, George thought how weird that there's a cemetery up there above us right now, bordered by multimillion-dollar beachfront properties. Prime real estate, occupied by bodies long dead and buried. Just now licked with tongues of light, there it was, in all of its eerie improbability: Waverley Cemetery. Flowers and weeds parked their way up the cliff face, peering at the graves above, roots fed by vegetal and animal decay. The names of the dead worn out on the gravestones, carved white angels tuning their faces cloudward, guards and guides above those who had been, been, yes, but not for years, decades, generations, old bones, dust-to-dust bones. Not enough angels, too many graves.

He was evidently doomed, or at least felt that way, those stone angels with their upturned eyes above him and dark bubbles below. Made his choice. Down. His muscles stayed working, warming, water still cold. That rioting buzz as he turned to see the swell — *Jesus, that's nice* — and he had his revenge on death and dying. He caught a wave which meant there was nothing else except this, this searing life and him in it.

Fizzled, caught one again, *Decent, yeah okay, not bad today, not bad.* His mori hardly needed another memento. From a young age George had known that the sea would be his way out, one day. Maybe this one. Maybe not.

The blue light was climbing quickly into blonde, and he felt expansive as a warm front. Best stay here, best stay quiet. Shrouded with water. Hermetic seal. His focus was interrupted by a wiry kid he knew from around, calling out 'Good karma, holy man!'

Legendary George: a still glowing if deteriorated surfer, even the haters secretly loved him.

The light had a sudden growth spurt. He could hear the forlorn murmurs of cars on the road above. A pointillist rendition of real life emerging as his head bobbed out of the water.

He got out, felt his shape returning to him, the

poor dimensions of a man. George felt lucky this particular man's dimensions were healthy, able, still fit. He scrolled his wetsuit down over his torso, perched on a rock, smelled burnt rubber. Or hair? Spotted a cluster of people down along the beach, wanted to see what they were all looking at.

As he got closer it looked all wrong. Unclear what was happening from afar, it was not much clearer close up. A ring of people stood around an object, another object, another again, washed up from the Pacific onto the beach. Big hunks of . . . meat? The fleshy mounds were four feet long or so and not human. They looked like giant tongues, the outer edge a sick grey, insides still pink with life, blood vessels and arteries. An onlooker held a border collie away, pulling tight on its red leash.

Whales ya think? What else could be that big? . . .

. . . But how did they get here?

Humpbacks in November . . .

Look like they've been torn right off . . .

What kind of augury was this? The smell turned on the wind and George left, flicking his hair, ridding it of water, God.

For all that was unclear about life, including his own, there were certainties in which George could take refuge, they included every crack and bump of the footpath that took him up to his semi-detached cottage, the letters crawling across the cement: CAMILLA + TRENT '01: these things were intimately known, like a beloved back-of-hand. His house, the shittiest place in Bronte with the best views in the world. The slap of his gate. The sign above the back door:

IN DOOM WE TRUST

Hiss of the sea beyond. The front yard, green-gold overgrown, the compost of broken chicken bones, oyster shells out back.

He pulled off his wetsuit and showered quickly outside, went in (door unlocked) and did the dishes. Yellow-gloved, deep breathing, trying to become one with a teacup.

His phone buzzed: *Paloma*. Like a gut punch.

He quickly pulled off the gloves, picked up the phone thinking a thousand things; of Paloma's hair falling over her face; Paloma, brighter than life; pale pink lips; black, black hair; Paloma, a no-longer familiar thrill. *Don't blow it*. Way too late for that.

'Hi.'

'Hey,' her voice was green, alive, and he fell in love with her again. 'How are you? How have you been? It's been . . . what . . .'

'I'm alright,' he said slowly, sighed.

'I know this is a bit awkward, me getting in touch out of nowhere. I need your help. I wouldn't have called but I've got no one else to ask.'

Wouldn't have called but . . .

'Two years,' George said, flicking on his kettle, which boiled companionably.

'What?'

'It's been two years since we've seen each other.'

'Feels like a lifetime.'

'You still angry at me?' he asked.

'No,' she said. 'I never was.'

'You should've been. Why are you calling?'

'There's . . . I think there's something wrong and I need help, in your professional capacity. There's this letter and it's really wigging me out. I can pay you of course.'

'Where are you these days?'

'I'm back up on Songbird Island for a bit. I don't want to say too much on the phone, I think it'd be better if you came up here so we could talk about it and I could show you the letter.'

George tapped his bare foot on the table. Watched the sunny garden blink with light. The kettle bubbled and shut itself off.

'Yeah, okay.' There were people he'd do anything for, anytime, and Paloma was one. Even now. Especially now.

'I want this to be professional, any other job, you know. I'll organise flights. How much does something like this cost?' she asked.

'Money isn't everything.'

But money talked and walked and bought an apartment in Double Bay and a clean new identity. Credit was personality. Cash ran through marrow. In his line of work. In his line of life.

'How about we talk about that when I get there.'

Songbird Island. He wondered if tourist season was in full swing yet. December? December. So yeah. He wondered if she was married. A kid? Two years was plenty of time. That'd be some fun to walk into.

After they goodbye-d, he slowly placed his phone

on the table between a paper bag of plums, a faded copy of *The Way of the Bodhisattva* and candles forlorn in the daylight, wicks frozen like accusing fingers.

———

GREEN INVESTIGATONS

He'd noticed the typo the moment the door painter had finished but he was too lazy, and more decisively, too broke, to fix it. When he started the business he felt certain that he needed a door with his name on it, and his logo, an open eye, underneath it, the frosted glass pixelating visitors into 8-bit. *No one gets these doors any more*, the painter had said. No refund for customer error, said his bill.

Nested above a vacant, oyster-coloured Darlinghurst shop — which had been in turn an empty-looking accountancy franchise, an empty-looking convenience store, and then just empty. Up two flights of narrow stairs, the office didn't inspire admiration; but it inspired a steady, nondescript assurance, which in his business was even better.

The space wasn't big. Wasn't quiet. It contained a hefty, scarred wooden desk, a filing cabinet, a complaining swivel chair, a better leather chair for the paying clients, walls the colour of blu-tac, a noisy and incompetent AC, a plastic drip-filter coffee machine, two windows dressed in muslin, a few hardcore potted palms, stacks of organised papers and George, who at this moment felt like a copy of a copy of his past self.

He wondered where his good shoes were. He

hadn't done much that required shoes at all lately. It was easy not giving a damn. That wasn't it, was it? Something always mattered. The sun always shone through his chick blinds in the morning. Darlinghurst yelped and demanded from his office window. The world walked through his misspelt door, wanting something or other. Usually other. And there it was again. Joy in being alive, or whatever you wanted to call it. Even during the worst bits, as during the most beautiful. He felt alive and grateful to be that way, temporary as it all was.

It wasn't the INVESTIGATONS. Well, not usually. The clients were generally messed up enough to think revenge would help them. Did he help them? Sometimes. They came to him at their most vulnerable, and sometimes there was what they would call a result. The occasional missing person found. Damages paid. It was a fragile happiness, one bought with too much pain. Skip tracing only when he was short on funds. No eye for an eye. Did a bit of a pro bono for a local law firm.

George shuffled through his active cases. A tired husband in Woollahra, Leichardt retiree scammed for savings, a basic background check, a discrimination case. All except the last were paid work, albeit not well. He sipped cold coffee and wondered, again, why he did any of it. He cared, and that's what it came down to, he supposed. He believed in karma; he was just helping it along. More importantly, the gig suited his temperament now that surfing was just for the thrills.

He googled *Songbird Island*, clicked 'News' scanned the headlines:

Legendary Songbird Island Developer Tom Knightley Dies, Age 85

Two Injured in Shark Attack Off Songbird Island

Paradise Lost? Knightley's Songbird and the End of an Era

He knew that Paloma's dad had died. He'd sent her a card and flowers, didn't feel she'd appreciate him sending himself. She'd replied with a short text, and George had responded politely, left dangling on read.

He googled: *Paloma Knightley.*

He found her Instagram. *Godhelpme.* Only verified her face was still beautiful. Beautiful sunsets. Beautiful European holidays. Beautiful men he didn't want to think about. Bitter as cloves. *Focus, George. Focus.*

Background check on the principles: Paloma Knightley, Celine Knightley, Celine's husband whatshisname. Paloma clean. Her sister Celine was irresponsible with her driving habits, inconsistent with her employment as a designer, not much else. One kid. One ex-husband. Current husband, Walter Eveleigh, a finance type, ex-UK, now an Australian permanent resident. Google images showed a broad-shouldered strawberry blond, if Van Gogh were a rugby player, polished next to Celine's sloe-eyed sophistication and organised hair.

Outside, Darlinghurst felt still and vacant, the buildings ghosting into the sky. What could the letter be? The Knightleys were a high-profile family. Cashed-up. Important. Blackmail? He leaned back in his chair which answered with a complaining creak. He felt unsettled. The electric night would roll on soon, the windows would turn smoky purple with dipping sun, and he listened, thinking, easing into the murmur of traffic and street.

2.

The bodies of tourists lay motionless on pure white sand.

It was a full-throated summer day, the sky stretching denim blue above a crystalline sea. The main beach on Songbird Island — protected by a crescent cove like a hand over a match — was made for pleasure. The kind of summer pleasure that dulled as it sharpened, heat making your marrow lazy as it sparked your senses.

Tourists in the shimmering heat wore bright streaks of bathing suits, exposing their lovely city-skin, their heads bobbing in the ocean, bodies splayed out motionless on the sand.

For Paloma the beach spoke of more particular pleasures. Of peach tans hot against cool linen sheets. Of ripe mango and chilled sparkling water, grasped with fingers gritted with sand. Of hair like a wet rope down her back. Of plunging, floating, losing all weight in the sea. It spoke of the cool opulence of the trade winds, dusting your eyelashes with sand. Of a young moon and stars collected in velvety black. Of being thrown by milky-crested waves when the wind picks up, laughing into the sky. Of short-lived rivalries in kayaks. Of the permissive world of holidays, where anything felt possible.

Paloma had known this beach her entire life, newborn to now. It didn't matter how old she was. She felt as ancient, and as inert, as a seam of opal. She was born on this spot, or more accurately, the house just beyond it. She'd heard the story plenty of times from her dad: how her mum had been night swimming, trying to ease her sore, swollen body, her pregnant heaviness lifting in the water; how Paloma was born warm and quick into sandy sheets, no time to get to the hospital on the mainland. *Always too keen to get where you're goin'*, her dad had said with a smile.

It felt good to be in the place she was born. Home. Where everything was touched with familiarity, a palimpsest of past under the present. Songbird Island was ghosted with past Palomas: the impatient newborn, the self-possessed child, the dreamy teenager, the ambitious twenty-something, the . . . whatever she was now. It felt good to sleep on her same bed, to hear the slow beat of the ceiling fan comforting in the night, the heartbeat of the house. Her room was the same as it always was. The dressing table was now populated with the bottles of a complicated skincare routine, but she could see it just as it was when she was a kid, crammed with books and toys and seashells; or as a teenager, loaded with photos and perfumes and fake red carnations.

Paloma welcomed the swinging light and summer breath of the island, found that her bones had longed for it. Home. She'd been away too long. She felt warm and private as an egg. What chuckling joy it was being beaten by the turquoise waves, their voice a soft whisper in the night. To feel, to smell that tropical rain, hard and then soft again. To watch the lightning flickering into the night from her window. To wake to a freshly made, orderly world. She was greedy for all of it.

She had come home and waited for her bravura to return, the embers of her to heat up again.

She walked the beach, espadrilles and a piece of paper hanging from her hand. She read over the letter for the maybe-sixtieth time, wind whipping it with sand. Glossy black words crawling over copy paper.

That man is guilty of serious wrongdoings against the Knightley family and its financial interests. He's been stealing from the company for years! Not to mention having affairs right under his wife's pretty nose. I have evidence that Mr Eveleigh has been embezzling millions to date, and who knows what he'll do now Old Mate is out of the way . . .

Who had written them? Why had they sent them to her? Other questions swam: When was the last time she'd seen George? Was she right to call him? Was any of it true, anyway? Would Walt really do any of it? Could he?

Home was home, golden, protected. This letter felt alien, a question in a place that had only ever given her answers.

———

Light-footed up the path, she found Celine waiting for her with coffee.

'*C'mon* Paloma,' Celine said impatiently.

'Oh thank God, coffee,' Paloma replied.

'Good morning to you too.'

Celine was always cool and alert at this hour — because she was a mother, Paloma supposed. She liked to see Celine cool and alert. Liked their daily morning walks.

As Paloma and Celine reached the promenade above the main beach, the sisters' voices were warm and close, the sun gathering courage.

Paloma said, 'George is coming up for a bit,' and watched as Celine sharpened all over.

'Do I need to remind you,' said Celine, 'that exes are exes for a very good reason.'

'No. You don't need to remind me.'

Paloma wasn't a natural liar, and this went doubly so when it came to her sister Celine, she always felt simpatico, the sisterly kind that didn't need words. Things were unchanged between them, even after the world had shifted since their father's death. They'd leaned into one another, relaxed into knowing, sure of one another always.

'You may have left *him*, technically, but the reality was that he left you. He gave you no choice. Which is worse. Cowardly.' Celine said.

'I remember,' Paloma said in a way that made Celine ease up. Though Paloma admired her sister's clarity on exes, remnants of love were forever, Paloma thought.

'But yes of course, he's welcome here,' Celine continued. 'When it comes to your own pleasure, who am I to judge?'

Celine was loyal if not faithful to her husband, Walt. To her, the distinction mattered. She had once said to Paloma: 'When the affair stops being pleasurable, you stop. Simple as that.' Celine always knew exactly what she wanted. Paloma admired her sister's clear-headed efficiency even if she didn't really understand it, and she certainly didn't judge it. Celine simply was. Next to her sister's cool sophistication, Paloma felt that her own relationships were hopelessly earnest.

Celine's men — well the husbands anyway — were always straightforward. They were either married or divorced. In love or out. What she lacked in monogamy she made up for in clarity: her men always knew exactly where they stood. She had been married twice, both times for love. The first in her extreme youth, barely eighteen — Paloma had never liked him — and the second, Walt, she didn't like much better. But Cee did, and that was what mattered.

'Surfing always came first, when you were together, you remember —'

'It's the same for all surf widows,' Paloma said. 'I knew that going in.'

'*Widows*,' echoed Celine. 'What does he do now anyway? Still surfing I suppose?' Celine's s's were taken off by the warm wind.

'No, he gave that up as far as I know. Professionally anyway.'

'He was so weird, but charismatic. Like a cult

leader. Exactly your type.' Celine smiled. 'So he's just dropping by, an old and dear friend.'

'Why not? Can we change the subject?'

'You brought it up. Of course he's more than welcome to stay as long as he likes. No, as long as *you* like. I'll kick him off the island if he's any trouble, we've got a whole security team, you just say the word. I'm actually glad to hear you feel like seeing people,' Celine said, softer.

But the image of George had emerged, conjured from the dark, and Paloma was distracted. The man had changed, no doubt: would his sunny skin be as cool and hard as a marble statue beneath her fingers? Would that smile still break like the sun through clouds? Images played hide-and-seek. In love or out? Out.

'I *don't* want to talk about men,' said Celine.

'Me either.'

'He *was* pretty hot though.'

Paloma laughed.

As they reached the house — what was it? Guilt? wouldn't shift and Paloma was afraid she would blurt something out just to fill the silence. She suddenly wished for a measure of luxuriant Celine calmness. She wished they'd talked about anything other than George.

As they neared the house a tropical rain came in thick and fast, and she took it as a blessing. The two women ran down the path and back inside, laughing, fat raindrops infused with sunlight making a din on the roof, as if the clouds were dropping diamonds.

—

'It's only getting worse, you know,' said Iris, watching the blurry horizon as the rain slowed, wearing a Missoni string bikini and a fuzzy halo of dun hair.

'Huge storm headed this way they're saying,' she continued, with tight excitement. 'Might even develop into a cyclone, can you imagine? A proper *emergency situation*.'

A smile curled on her lips. Iris was never really warm or moved by much, even from the earliest days when they were all kids and she used to come to stay on the island for endless school holidays. She had been back on the island for a few months now and the years had yawned in between, insignificant.

Iris hadn't stayed close to Paloma or any of the family especially, but when her husband went missing in Melbourne, with apparently no warning and no leads, Iris had been at a loss. Her own parents were now in the States, and she'd remembered those warm summer holidays with their festive tranquillity, Paloma supposed, and asked Cee if she could come up and stay for a while. The vast house had swallowed her whole.

'Nothing to worry about,' Paloma said. 'Life as usual in the sub-tropics.'

Iris was always self-contained, and her slate eyes looked at Paloma in a way that made Paloma gulp down her natural curiosity and the majority of her sympathy.

'I'm off for a swim. I suppose that's safe for now,' Iris said, and left.

It was fine, Paloma thought, to be self-contained, cold, even a bit aggressive. Iris had her moods, as they all did: the heart has its limits. Grief works in obscure ways.

Paloma moved into the front living room and noticed that Iris had left her thick towel and her phone on the lounge, so she picked them up thinking to catch her on the path to the beach. At that moment the phone vibrated, a message in emerald on Iris's home-screen:

> NOBODY ☺
>
> 8 tomorrow, usual place

Paloma wondered who else Iris knew on the island, but hesitated to ask her directly. They weren't icy, not exactly, neither were they close. They'd never been the type to talk about matters of the heart, and Paloma didn't want to ask now and risk sounding like a spy. Iris came back through the door, breathless, smiling with her pretty, sharp little teeth.

'Oh I just realised I'd forgotten my . . .' she took the phone and towel from Paloma, with a glance at the phone, which was still illuminated. 'Thanks babes.'

—

Paloma had been two, Celine four, when their mother died. Paloma's memories of that time weren't real things, they were photographs on the walls, collapsing reality into yellow-toned snapshots, showing a woman Paloma didn't remember or know.

Paloma looked at the photos in her dad's study and wondered which memories, unphotographed, had been lost forever now? Photographs burned neural pathways. Was that why she'd turned to photography? To capture life, create memories, before they inevitably fled?

She wondered: *If I hadn't been born and raised here, how different would I be?*

This place was straightforwardly paradise. Paloma had been born warm into the world and the world was warm for her. It was a world of ease, opulence, one of blood-love and money. Even death, when it came to her mum, hadn't really touched Paloma.

For as long as long, it was Paloma-Cee-Dad. A bubble in the bubble of the island. Her father was kind and loving — sad sometimes too — but kind above all. The limits of her childhood world were uncomplicated. The island was so long, so wide, and Paloma's kayak (or her bravery) could only take her so far away from it.

It was the hotel kitchen, pilfering a doughnut and sandwich triangle and running off laughing with Cee; it was the height of Dad's china cabinet stocked with curiosities: glinting astrolabes, weird herbaria; later it was as high as Founders Peak, as deep as their scuba dives in Priests Bay.

It hadn't occurred to her until much later that the island *belonged* to her family. It occurred only later again how shameful that was. To own an island.

Had the place shaped her in meaningful ways? It was only a question of extent.

The island and her family were intertwined, but the island itself (pop. 1229) had its own stories. Of fate and fatality, mostly; those sorts of stories run through remote communities like a shiver. Of the colonists with their piercing ships getting the date wrong. Should technically be The Whitmondays. Stories of genius loci. Of escape.

One visitor, in the late seventies, had sought refuge on Songbird Island. When escape was still possible here. Paloma tried to imagine it, an emerald forested island with no airport, no hotel, no roads, no permanent population: just the suede of deep green forest and sweep of white sand, dotted in the bright endless sea. He was a famous race-car driver named David Bell, and he was dying. He travelled to the island from America, because sometimes as far away as possible is the only distance that makes sense. He paid handsomely, built a compound, long since demolished, he gathered his people, and he waited to meet death. Paloma always felt that his energy had stayed in the place even after he'd gone. She'd read about him, about his beautiful wife, about his famous, tragic life, how he'd died just as her dad was developing the island, and for whatever reason he felt present to her.

One idle night as a teenager, she wondered about him. Had it given him the peace he had travelled so far to find? Did he come to terms, as much as any man could, with his own death? That night, lying atop her millefleur quilt not-sleepy, hot and late she had whispered into the night:

David Bell. If you're here, make yourself known. Give me a sign.

The power immediately went out across the island.

Hi, nice of you to come: Paloma said over the beating of her heart in her throat, because it would be rude not to answer after she asked.

You can put the lights back on if you like.

The lights had come back on again.

In the night-dark room, these many years later, Paloma wondered if she'd ever have the strength of heart to say those same words to her dad, to her mum, to see what kind of hello they'd give her. She wondered too, if she'd die here too.

How stupid, she thought. Her heart beat hard in her chest.

———

George smelled like a New Age shop in a seaside town: sea salt, sunscreen, patchouli incense.

Bright birds swooped overhead as Paloma and George, ex-couple, came together once again in the inauspicious surrounds of the island's airport car park. The particulars of George, human, were as familiar as ever to Paloma, like a sentence from a book that kept running through your head. She quickly catalogued the changes: shorter beard, shorter hair — some grey some dark some sun-coloured — utterly charming crow's feet, a hollow down his cheeks, like someone had pulled a knife softly over butter. And how he looked at her! The smile still broke like sunrise. Atoms spoke to atoms, it wasn't intellectual, and Paloma felt very much alive. And in trouble.

She remembered a time, when they were still together, when a mate of George's said to him: *Pal is beautiful, but don't tell her. She's beautiful because she doesn't really know it.* George had told Paloma, naturally, and it had struck her as such an odd compliment: as if women didn't know early on what kind of currency beauty was with men, as if they weren't made aware of their own credit or deficit at a young age.

George's beauty was not of the unaware kind. His arms, eyes, the way he moved, it all knew the power of seduction, knew that he was attractive, that he was capable, his cells fully charged, fizzing, alert. What was wealth, fame, looks, compared to that? He had always been aware of his own shortcomings too, all too willing to acknowledge when he fucked up, how fucked the world was, and he still gave off that same impression. A downbeat bodhisattva.

3.

George was hit by a green scent that was as much the island as Paloma as she came in close and warm to hug him; it was beautiful, and it was painful. They were in love again, he supposed. Or he was.

'You got rid of the beard!' Paloma said. 'You've changed.'

'And you're exactly the same.'

'I don't feel the same at all.'

They walked through the car park, the insect sounds of golf buggies around them, an idling mini-bus waiting to take the tourists to the main hotel. Attendees circled in short-legged navy uniforms. They arrived at Paloma's ivory MG, George threw his bag into the back and once his bare legs touched the red leather, they were instantly sticky.

The road was quilted with plant life on either side, snug as they drove towards the house. George's eyes glided over everything: Paloma's thighs, yachts flashing in the turquoise water below, then the main beach sheltered by a forested cove, bungalows and the resort buildings nested in the green, split occasionally by aqua pools and sandy slices of road.

'Cee's been busy making changes to the resort,' Paloma said, 'a meditation garden, yoga studio, all her hippie shit, you'll love it.'

'I'm not very interested in Celine right now,' George said.

Paloma's laugh was the same. 'You liar. You're interested in every single person in the world.'

'I'm interested in *you*.'

They drove past jetties moored with pearlescent yachts, sails shimmering in the heat.

'You still doing photography?'

'Not so much right now. On a break from work for the rest of the year,' she said.

What a stunning world this was, George thought, hit with it, feeling as if Darlinghurst and Bronte beach and tired husbands and quick-witted lawyers and walking money and junkies and all the sadnesses of the city were melting away and this, the warm wind and tranquil sea and forested mountains and Paloma's dark eyes were everything there ever was. Paloma's whole life was a holiday. As they drove past the main hotel, a cherry-red sign caught his eye:

WELCOME TO PARADISE

Quick eyes took in artefacts that cost more than George's entire house. Paloma's dad's domain, through and through. He liked a curio, Tom did, the man universally known as Old Mate. George had liked Tom when they'd met years before, liked his plump good-natured face, his endless bon mots. Tom had looked at Paloma and Cee with a pride and an unshakeable, protective sort of love that it had hit George in the gut. How many people had looked at him like that? Later, too late, he also wondered: how many people had *he* looked at like that?

A spiral staircase dominated the heart of the Knightley family home, stretching up to a vast domed skylight. Huge palms stood between mahogany furnishings, a wooden daybed, stands topped with heavy white lamps. Countless other rooms behind white plantation-shutter doors. Mediterranean blue, dark wood, blinding white.

As they entered the main foyer, a tall, black-haired man was passing through to the front door. His hair was pushed back, accentuating a widow's peak and grey-blue eyes pocketed in finely wrinkled flesh. He moved gracefully, his linen shirt unbuttoned in a deep V. George wondered idly how someone stayed so pale in this place. He wasn't handsome, with his weak chin and lank hair. He had a wiry, animal sexiness — George's gut told him to pay particular attention to him.

'Hey Adam,' said Paloma.

'Oh hey,' he replied, 'What are you up to? Do you want to come down to the marina? Your brother-in-law is demanding a boozy lunch,' he spoke in a way that was self-aware, almost performative.

'Sounds about right. I think we'll pass. I'll settle George in, give him the tour.'

'What can I say, it's a hard life,' Adam glanced at George with pointed curiosity.

'Adam, this is my old friend George, he's staying with us for a bit. George, Adam,'

'Hey man,' said George, and they shook hands briefly, each taking the other's measure.

'I'm Walt's assistant.'

'Oh you're practically one of the family these days. Feels like you've been here forever,' Paloma said, but there wasn't much enthusiasm in her voice.

'Is that a good thing?' A lopsided, gratified smile appeared on his lips. 'I guess I'll need a name change then if you're adopting me. Adam Eveleigh. Or should it be Adam Knightley?'

'I'm biased but Knightley sounds more regal.'

'Regal? Eveleigh it is for me then,' he smiled. 'Anyway. Walt will be starting without me, and that never ends well. Come across if you both change your mind,' he said, leaving them alone.

As they climbed up the multicoloured tiles of the stairs to George's room the skylight let in waves of light, bouncing off a complex chandelier the size of a small boat.

About the size of his Bronte place, his room was warm and light and airy, filled with birdsong. George circled the room, poking his head into the ensuite and walk-in wardrobe, watched the blinking blue sea beyond the shutters, felt poorer.

'Let's go for a swim,' he said to Paloma, eager to be out on the beach. More familiar territory. The great equaliser.

Outside, the family house loomed, with its wide sea-facing verandah, decked balcony with balustrades, commanding the best view of the main and most beautiful beach, tip to tip.

'Are you with anyone?' Paloma asked, once they were in the water. George was surprised, showed it.

'I'm . . . no, I'm not in love with anyone.' He thought: except you. He said nothing.

'I'm being nosy,' she said, 'But it's a bit of an elephant in the er, sea, between us, so I thought best to get it out of the way. I'm not either. In love.' He smiled despite himself.

They swum out and their legs were circling in the clear water and were both feeling easy and complex. The ocean had a way of making the most profound human emotions seem smaller.

They swam back in, racing, and stretched on the white silica sand of the beach, drying off almost instantly. They bought peaches and a glass bottle of sparkling water from the beachside kiosk, eating silently together on their towels. *Why do I suddenly feel perfect?* thought George. He knew, and he still wasn't sorry he'd come.

He wanted words to express those thoughts as they dangled in his mind, but it would be unfair on Paloma to try to grasp them, give them form, so instead he said, 'So about this letter.'

Paloma collected her thoughts for a long moment. 'It's probably nothing,' she said. 'But I didn't know who else to talk to. Believe it or not, I don't know a lot of private detectives.'

'Nothing can really surprise me any more. I've heard it all.' he replied.

'I received a weird letter last week. It's clearly from someone who knows us, the family I mean, knows Walt and Cee and the business. They're claiming some pretty serious things. A warning, they say. Mostly about Walt.'

'What does it say about Walt?'

'Probably best to read it yourself. It's back at the house. It says he's been embezzling money from the family business, which is ridiculous. It also claims he's been cheating on Cee, which is . . . if I'm honest, and this is just between us, less ridiculous.'

'Do they ask for anything?'

'That's the weird bit. Well, the other weird bit. Not a thing. It says it's just a friendly warning.'

'How selfless. You don't think there's any truth to the embezzlement stuff?'

'I don't see why he would. They've been married for years. They both have more money than they know what to do with really, even more now Dad's gone. We all do, though none of us care about it. He's been in the family business for almost two decades. No, I don't believe it.'

'So why am I here?'

'Who sent it? And why? It's probably best to make sure Walt isn't doing anything shady, right?'

'Right.'

—

Paloma sat cross-legged on the bed watching George silently, both with lots of tanned skin and Paloma in espadrilles and white cotton. He held the letter.

Ms Knightley,

I am not a snitch but I feel I must do as conscience compels me, not to mention the law, and come forward now, and I hope you understand why I've done so under the cloak of anonymity.

Look, my reasons for not coming forward are many, but circumstances now force my hand. The passing of Mr Knightley is a tragedy for all of us. I'm deeply afraid that now he's 'out of the way', the serious wrongdoings that have been perpetrated by certain parties will escalate beyond what form of control Mr Knightley's existence until now has hampered.

Now listen closely! Walter Eveleigh is a con man! That man is guilty of serious wrongdoings against the Knightley family and its financial interests. He's been stealing from the company for years! Not to mention having affairs right under his wife's pretty nose. I have evidence that Mr Eveleigh has been embezzling millions to date, and who knows what he'll do now Old Mate is out of the way. These are not just rumours or suspicions. Again, I've seen the evidence with my own eyes. I'm afraid of losing my position I hope you understand. I tell you, with Knightley gone he will only do worse, and the time's come for me to speak out. I assure you, you'll find a man of worse character than any of you realise, he needs to be stopped for the good of the company, and your family. It's been going on for many years.

A Friend.

George looked over it carefully, front, back,

envelope, seal, before speaking. 'When did you get this?'

'A few days before I called you. The Tuesday I think.'

'Who got it out of the mailbox?'

'I don't know. It was on the hall stand, where the mail usually is whenever anyone gets it in from the main hotel.'

'Any signs it had been opened?'

'No.'

'The island's head office is in Sydney, right?'

'Yes.'

'Who do you think sent it?'

'An employee from the sound of it. Who else would know all that?'

'Why would they send it to you? Not the board of directors. Not Celine. You, specifically.'

'The best I can guess is that this person has more faith in our family than anyone else in the business, I mean Walt's heavily involved in the day-to-day business after all, so that sort of makes sense. And maybe they didn't want to upset Cee, so . . .'

'Could anyone have something personally against Walt?

'Any number of people I'd imagine.'

'Yourself included?'

'No. Walt loves Celine. She loves him. I don't have to like him.'

'You wouldn't choose Walt for her though, would you?'

'No one gets to choose who they love.'

'So, what about him having an affair, you say it's likely?'

'I wouldn't be surprised, I don't know though. I hope not.'

'Who have you told about the letter?'

'No one. I couldn't tell Cee, of course. Who's to say any of this is true? She has enough going on.'

George sat in thought, hesitating.

'What is it?' Paloma asked.

'Don't take it the wrong way if I'm short with you, or ask confronting questions, or seem distant, or weird. It's part of the job you've hired me for, that's it.'

'I get it.'

'As you said, it could be nothing at all. Sometimes things like this are a hoax, a troublemaker doing what they do, or someone who just wants a payout. Either way, I'm here, this is my job, I do it every day. I'll find out the truth, and whatever it is we'll deal with it together. Are you Facebook friends with everyone who's living in the house right now?'

'I guess so. Yes . . . Except for Jude, my nephew, he won't friend anyone from the family. Why?'

'Just ruling people out,' he said.

4.

Just ruling people out. Paloma wandered down the main path, leaving George back in the house. She was achingly aware that she was alive on a beautiful evening in the place she knew best, the sky full and tender, the guy who broke her heart metres away in her house. This was *her place.* The cotton-wool thunderstorms, the hanging fruit of the beach cherry trees, the salt-heavy smell of the ocean and zing of ozone. Even the tourists she passed, their foreheads slick with sweat, from Adelaide, Sydney, Melbourne, Brisbane, overseas, were as much a part of her family, her sense of belonging, as anything else here. For a blissful moment that mattered.

She had wanted to tell George on the beach, *I'm not the same person I was,* but the distance felt too great to say what she meant. None of that felt possible, neither pretending to be her old self, or letting him in to see the new Paloma. How could she put any of it in to words to him, he who she used to know her better than anyone else, now a parenthesis to her life?

Now there was this letter, this nagging suspicion, and George was here reminding Paloma of a self that she thought was gone forever. One who loved deep and was loved in return, was all in, the Paloma before the heartbreak. Was that a good thing or a bad thing?

She breathed in deeply as she approached the day spa, a big, serene, secluded building with a water-sided entrance tucked away beyond the cove, shining in polished wood and chuckling streams, a place of carefully rolled towels, herbed oils, and expensive quiet.

She didn't know exactly why she'd come, and why she'd brought her camera, perhaps it was George's influence — he was investigating the letter, why not do a little investigating of her own? What was it about Iris that made her feel so uneasy?

Paloma found a spot near the buggy path, across from the spa's main entrance, and felt self-conscious as she glanced about to see if anyone was watching her, before crouching into the bushes, her telephoto lens resting on top of her knee.

What am I doing, she laughed quietly at herself. She checked the time: 7.41 pm. Well, she thought, I'm here now. Itchy. But here.

She waited. It shouldn't have surprised her, because Paloma knew Iris would be coming. Her heart dropped as she watched through the lens as Iris approach the spa, sliding the door open quickly. *She has a keycard.* Paloma squeezed the shutter. She waited, breathless, panicky. She was not cut out for this.

Soon after, a man's figure approached the door, slipping in with a keycard of his own. A dark-haired man. An unmistakable man: Adam.

She snapped more photos as he went in too.

Paloma wondered if she should try to get closer, but she wouldn't be able to see anything from the front. She then wondered if she should tell George or not. Would it be relevant? She quickly stood and went back to the house, and went to her room to think things through.

A tryst? I mean, why not? They're both single.

If Iris sought comfort after her own husband had left — and who knew exactly what had gone on there — who could blame her? Adam was attractive enough, in his own unwholesome, possibly diseased way. It could be a good diversion for her. Maybe for Adam, who certainly had eyes for Cee, maybe Walt too, neither of whom were good for his future prospects. Or were they? Why would they keep it a secret? Who would really care?

Back at the house, Paloma made herself a negroni from the bar cart in her room. Something to do, and maybe it would dull the pain in her head. Dad hadn't liked having alcohol around the house, so she still felt some residual teenager guilt about it. Her habits were all different here. *Too much unoccupied time on your hands isn't good*, her therapist had frowned, *the brain eats itself.* Was her brain eating itself? She didn't think so. Paloma hadn't thought about her therapist much, now she wasn't seeing her every week. Paloma didn't feel worse here on the island. Or better. She still caught her mind going to unhealthy places, focusing on the smallest physical sensations and blowing them out of proportion with illogical speculation. Yet she felt swallowed up by the familiarity of the island, and for the first time in many months, she could forget from time to time. She forgot to label thoughts as her therapist had taught her, she forgot to catastrophise at all. She just *was*.

She sipped the negroni. Her therapist had urged her to text whenever she felt the urge to google physical symptoms, to stay accountable. She was no longer her therapist anymore, and Paloma needed to know, just this one last time. She googled: *symptoms brain aneurysm.*

While she scrolled, Paloma's phone buzzed with a text from KJ. A grey-haired Croatian chef with an amazing face. Sort of seeing one another, sort of not, for the last year or so. She was too old to be any sort of sort of, yet here they were. She wouldn't commit, his life was full, so he never pressed. He called her 'kiddo'. But then he also had that face. He was busy enough, his hours wild enough, his independence strong enough, that Paloma's lack of presence was nothing more than convenient.

> Hey cutie, you coming back to Sydney for Lia's bday thing?

> Not sure yet

> Come!!! I need to see you. Come to mine before. Or after. Stay over a few nights.

> How have you been?

Paloma didn't know how to answer that question. She didn't want to think about answering that question. She watched the three dots blinking.

> We have Lia to thank, after all, for us meeting one another. I miss you

> Send me a photo xxx

She realised that she hadn't thought of KJ much since she'd left Sydney, outside of when he texted or called after his shifts, her sleepy, him wired. She liked him, liked kissing him, liked his hands, the way they handled food: tender, light, respectful. The way they handled her. But when he was gone it was as if he had been an apparition.

She thought about sitting on the beach earlier with George. The ease of it. How she'd tried not to look at him, at that place where his swim shorts sat on his hips, the division between his deeply tanned skin and the clear white she knew was just beyond, between public and private.

With George all she had to do was think of him, and it was almost as if he were in the room with her, conjured complete. His smell, his voice, his touch. She knew it wasn't at all fair of her to compare the love of her life — if that's what George was — with someone she'd been casually seeing for a . . . well, more than a little while now. She sighed.

> I miss you too.

5.

George opened his laptop. You got to know some interesting characters in his line of work. Dr Beringer was one of them.

He slipped on headphones, a pixellated version of Dr Beringer's face materialised in the FaceTime window.

'Doc,' he said. Though she was little more than a sand-and-blonde-coloured-shape, he could smell the musty sour of her closed-in office, filled with books, that reassuring office with its desk fan, its bureaucratic beige furniture. Imagined himself sliding down the 1970s university halls. For a high school dropout, it had an air of mystery and romance.

'Hey George. What can I do for you?' she said.

'I need your linguistic expertise. I have a specimen for you to take a look at.'

'Sounds good to me, you've actually rescued me from the perils of marking. I'd much rather get stuck into a little forensic linguistics if I'm honest. Students are such dweebs. So what have we got?'

'It's anonymous tip-off letter, fairly meaty.'

'Meaty! Good. And for comparison?'

'Not too much right now, some Facebook profiles to start you off.'

'Better than nothing. Send them over, I'll take a look.'

'What can I do for you? Need me to look into any of the dweebs' excuses for missing deadlines? Dead grandmas to verify?'

'Ha! No, I'll give them the benefit of the doubt. Like sleeping dogs, it's better to let students lie.'

'You're too lenient.'

'And you're too tough. Always after justice.'

'Professional hazard.'

'You're the least professional person I know, George. Which is saying a lot as someone from academia. The first time I met you, I don't think you were wearing pants . . .'

'They're overrated.'

'True. I do have this nasty habit of wearing them to class. What are you doing anyway? You still working that pro bono case?'

'Yeah.'

'Don't worry. I won't tell anyone.'

'I'll email you now Doc. Be well.'

'You too George.'

The screen cut to black.

—

Oversized wooden windows let in glimpses of the mercurial sea, while Old Mate watched over proceedings from a life-sized portrait, somewhere in the vicinity of sixty, George thought as he waited in the dining room. Glinting oils, a shadow cutting through the older man's worn face, a generously proportioned stomach. They got the determined, yet kind look right. Like a dog with a bone, George thought. Or a minor deity.

About my daughter. She's from a loving family. Even if it hasn't been a complete one, it's a protective one, he'd said to George the first time they had met.

White gauzy curtains fluttered, concealing and revealing the distant view of green trees and blue sea. George was showered and as neat as he got in a fresh shirt and a combed beard. He stood up, eyed the big terracotta urn underneath the portrait of Old Mate. Wondered. Stuck his hand in. Empty.

The room was full of ghosts and he wanted more material companions. He relaxed into himself, breathing deep, as he settled into gut-mode. Ready to study them. He didn't wait long.

'We don't do this every night,' Paloma said, gliding in looking so beautiful he wanted to punch something. 'Family dinner I mean. I wish we would though.'

'No, it's entirely for your benefit,' said another, similar voice behind her, Celine, wearing a black silk dress that floated around her like expensive smoke. She had a gaze that could gutter candles, or at least, men.

'I remember *you*,' she said, enclosing George in a hug, folding him in a cloud of exotic, dangerous perfume.

'You're looking well Celine,' he said (she was).

'And you got more handsome,' she said (which he

had, depending who you ask), 'as men sometimes do. Those cheekbones look like they come with magic powers.'

'Oh *you* haven't done too badly yourself, Celine,' said Iris, who had come in too, holding a lipstick-mooned wineglass. 'How old are you now anyway? You don't look a day over thirty . . . five.'

'Oh, I've been kicking around for eons,' said Celine, pouring herself a wine, undisturbed by the question. 'I'm actually quite looking forward to being old.'

'You already *are old*,' said a male voice sweetly, as a young man who could be none other than Celine's teenage son Jude joined them at the table.

'I mean *really* old,' continued Celine. 'A crone. A hag.'

'It'll suit you somehow,' said Paloma.

'I take that as a compliment,' Celine replied, satisfied. 'Crone energy is powerful.'

They were soon joined by Adam, intensely black hair curling in Cs around his ears. He sat next to Iris. He was dressed in slim-cut pants and a clinging T-shirt, bare ankles and suede shoes.

Last to arrive was Walt, a thick-shouldered strawberry blonde with good skin and a bad mood. He had an air of crispness that was partly the effect of his neatly tucked shirt and wet-combed hair, part genetic, part the way he moved.

'You must be Paloma's friend,' he said, shaking George's hand briskly, before sitting at the head of the table. 'Welcome, make yourself at home and all that.' As he sat under the portrait his cool look couldn't have been more different than ready-to-smile eyes of Old Mate.

Father and son, sitting next to one another; both looked a little cramped in their chairs, but that was where their similarities ended. Jude's hot feline grace and mother's dark eyes contrasted starkly with the glacial constraint of the older man.

George breathed in and out slowly and let the overall atmosphere of the place take over, let his instinct swim in the sensation of being in that room, awash with expressions, spoken and not. When he investigated, and make no mistake, he was investigating now, there were moments when it was necessary to be simply conscious, to get fuzzy and loose and diffuse. Now, he wanted to understand the house and the people in it with a sense that wasn't reason. He watched gently, unattached to the scene.

'So what's the latest on this so-called cyclone?' asked Iris, addressing no one in particular. She had the sudden movements of a bird, giving her a nervy, excited air.

'No so-called, not anymore,' said Walt. 'Cyclone Lucie. The system has been officially upgraded, gale-force winds hitting here tomorrow ahead of her. Just a cyclone right now though, not severe.'

'Any chance it's coming our way?' asked Iris.

'Could do. We'll have to wait and see,' Walt replied, bored. 'Where's the food? I'm starving.'

'These things can change in a flash,' said Celine, reaching for a bread roll. 'It will likely pass us by completely.' There was something opulent about

Celine, the self-possession of someone comfortable in their metier. Something secretive, too, in the way she brushed her hair, the humour behind her eyes. A witchy *knowing*.

'But what happens if it does head our way?' continued Iris, drinking from her deep wine glass, re-filling.

'If we're really in danger we'll know with plenty of time in advance. They'll evacuate the island if it looks really bad,' said Celine.

'Evacuate . . .' repeated Iris.

'Have you ever had to evacuate before?' asked Jude, mouth full of bread.

'A few times when we were little,' said Paloma. 'It was all an adventure, though, remember Cee? The island was never too badly damaged.'

'Let's hope it doesn't come to that,' said Celine. 'I like my bed.'

'Hear, hear. Just think of all the money you'd lose, not to mention the bad publicity,' said Adam.

'Paloma said you've given up surfing?' Celine asked, focusing on George in a way that suggested he was the only person in the world.

'I still surf, just not professionally.'

'Sports are funny like that,' said Adam. 'You're over it, a retiree by the time you're thirty.'

'So what do you do now? As a retiree?' Celine smiled.

'Let me guess!' said Iris with a smile. She looked at him, eyes slitting. 'A prize-fighter?'

'Not quite,' he replied.

'A priest!'

'Closer. I coach surfers now, teach the little ones what's what.' he said.

'I'd like to learn to surf,' said Jude.

'Come by when you're in Sydney,' George replied.

Adam was looking down at his glass as if it were whispering him prophecies. Was he out of sorts? Or always this way?

At that moment dinner was served by kitchen staff wearing neat cream and navy, shimmering in with immense silver platters. *House staff*, thought George, embarrassed for himself and everyone on Earth.

'Wild barramundi with coconut cream, tomato masala and Vietnamese mint,' said a man as he unveiled one of the trays.

It smelled, and then tasted, delicious.

'So what are you doing while you're here?' Adam asked George as they ate.

'Right now I'm on a break,' he said.

'We're all on a break,' said Jude. 'No one does anything around here as far as I can tell.'

'Hey! I work for a living. You speak for yourself,' Adam threw a bread roll at him in response, Jude ducked.

'Children, please,' said Celine. Celine looked at Adam with an indulgent smile, and Adam looked satisfied at her. Iris sighed loudly. Another little electric shock.

George looked over at Paloma: she gulped her wine, then cut her food up into very small pieces, very slowly, not eating a bit of it. It was an action that was completely unlike her, or the Paloma he knew, and

George tucked this information away for later, wondering what it meant. Maybe nothing. He tried not to focus on it. Too much else to take in.

'What are you doing tomorrow?' Celine asked her sister.

'No plans yet.'

'Let's go diving. George will love it. George, do you dive?'

'Now and then. Not for a long while though. Sounds great,' he said, but couldn't help but notice Paloma — Paloma who had loved few things more than being under the sea — was again reticent, studying her food. What was going on with her?

'Paloma?'

'Yeah sounds good,' she said, the smile not reaching her eyes.

'I'm in,' said Jude.

'Take *Chakra* out,' said Walt. 'I'll have it re-stocked tonight.'

After dinner everyone evaporated, plates and trays vanished, and the group moved in small clusters to different parts of the house. George wandered outside onto the porch, the heavy tinkling of cutlery behind him.

The air was light as gauze, the sky blue velvet, pricked with first stars. George sat and thought of Paloma — the smell and the quick grace of her and the way she had been over dinner with the food and her despondency, and despite the utopia in front of him, he felt burdened. A text came through: Dr B.

Call me when you get a sec.

'How's life, doctor?' he asked, wandering away from the house and down to the beach.

'You really should call me Nadine. But you won't.'

'You worked hard to be a doctor, you should get thrills from it.'

'Oh, yeah, my life is full of thrills . . . especially compared to yours.'

'You don't want my kind of thrills,' he said. 'I don't even want them.'

'I don't feel sorry for you,' she replied, 'You get the bad guys, isn't that how it works? Simple.'

'I wish it were that simple. Sometimes the bad guys don't really even exist.'

'Depends on what you think of as bad, I suppose,' she said. 'How about this one particular bad guy? The one related to the letter. How's it going with him or her?'

'Slowly. I'm hoping that you have something more solid for me to go on.'

'Well, I do and I don't. The letter itself had several distinguishing linguistic markers, which made the job easier. The contractions in particular . . .'

'Explain it slow to me, like I'm a private detective,' he said.

'Well, almost everyone commonly uses both sorts of contractions, positive and negative. For example, "I wasn't there," is a negative contraction, "Yes, I'm going to be there," is positive.

'In the letter, the writer sometimes used positive contractions, but never contracted negative verbs. They wrote "I am not a snitch" for example, and "This is not a joke" —yet their positive verbs are contracted, "I've done so," "I've got strong reason" and so on.

'Now, is there any reason to suspect anything untoward in the death of this Mr Knightley?'

'Tom?' George asked, taken aback. 'No. None at all.'

'The letter refers to him as "out of the way" twice, and once uses quotation marks, which suggests the author is focusing your attention here, insinuating something else is going on. But perhaps not.

'The other thing that stands out is a certain sense of the dramatic. Writing it under a "cloak of anonymity" and so on.

'Then there's the asterismos. Very distinctive! That's all about the use of unnecessary words and introductions, it's the way we draw attention to whatever we've got to say. So, things like "listen" and "firstly" and that kind of thing. Whoever is reading is already paying attention, so it's semantically pointless. Rhetorically, however, asterismos subconsciously points to what you're about to say, giving it gravitas. Whoever wrote this letter *loves* a bit of asterismos. You'll notice they often write "now listen closely", "I'm telling you", "look" and other similar phrases to start their sentences. It's actually quite unusual.'

'All this is sounding great,' George said, 'but you know what my next question is going to be —'

'Yes. And I have a caveat. I've analysed those Facebook feeds and any associated social media I could get my hands on, and compared them to the letter, and while there *is* a link to a certain person's social media prose style, I would be remiss if I didn't mention the fallibility of social media as a forensic linguistic analysis tool.'

'I understand.'

'This is not incontrovertible evidence, George. Yes, everyone has a unique linguistic fingerprint so to speak, we all have habits and styles that together make our linguistic identity. But there are significant differences between social media and a letter like this one. Informality, abbreviation, slang, emojis and sarcasm are all native to Facebook, but not in a printed letter like this, which is more formal. Any connections we draw based solely on social media are at the most, tenuous. I'd need another sample, that's not social media based, to confirm it. Can you get one?'

'I'll sure as hell try,' he said. 'As for the caveat, I very much acknowledge it. Who's the closest match?'

'Adam.'

———

George was alone while the dark bent around the corners of his room, gradually enveloping the hard edges of the furniture until everything was soft and indistinct.

He didn't go after suffering, not any more. Here it was anyway, all there in Paloma's face, all the things he'd fucked up and the biggest of fuck-ups: losing her. There still wasn't anyone but her. No other hearts but Paloma's to break.

I forgive you, he said, a mantra in the dark.

I forgive you.

I forgive you.

But it wasn't his own forgiveness he was after.

Who was she now? Had she changed? As a private eye, he'd looked as hard and objective as he could when they were driving, swimming, talking; hunting clues. Same face, infinitely beautiful. Maybe sadder. A new henge of freckles under her right eye. More careful in her movements. More tense? Cautious? No . . . what was it? Fear. She looked, if George was right, afraid of something. What? And the way she'd been at dinner, that was new. Her body still spoke to his and the things they said were indisputable, gorgeous, wrong. He felt heavy as a wet towel.

George still loved her, he knew that; with the battered love of something that has been habitually confined. He felt selfish. Being witness to her he had never felt more like a tourist. Her thoughts looked deeper than his, darker. She was thinking of something important — and here he was feeling the personal loss of her skin, hair, lips, his own happiness, wondering if she'd ever take him back, or have a fling while he was there, or at the very least sleep with him once more, goddammit he'd even be okay if she just kissed him.

Being here, it hit him again just how loaded she was. Big family money. The kind that glides over everything and everyone. That evens out bumps and removes surprises.

He'd first realised how wealthy Paloma was after they'd been seeing each other for a few months. *Come apartment hunting with me,* she had said. All the people George had known in this world had share-housed, or rented; those few who bought their own houses were usually pro-surfers, cashed up and ready to spend, or managed to lock down utter shitboxes with the help of their parents. So when they arrived at the apartment she was looking at, he was breathless. Water views in the heart of moneyed Vaucluse. The place was gigantic. He fell quiet as they walked through the house, its deck, its cool, tiled bathroom, the shadow of the agent in the kitchen trilling marketing epithets. *Three point five,* the agent had said. George wondered how he'd never suspected it before. Afterwards in the car, she asked him what he thought of it. *It's beautiful,* he had said, and *don't buy it.*

Why not?

Move in with me instead.

And to his surprise, she'd said yes.

At one time George had wanted all of it: money, fame, love, sex, highs of all kinds, everything that came with his idea of success. Everything he had never had before. Then he got some of each, and he realised why they warned you to be careful what you wished for.

—

Paloma's teeth flashed in bright sunlight. They were bobbing on the ocean, on the family's yacht named *Chakra* — 'Cee's idea,' Paloma laughed. The sea was clean as a diamond, the horizon softened with fleecy cumulus.

'What you thinking about?' he asked her.

'Nothing.'

Above was endless blue, below deck was all warm amber, emerald velvet, and polished wood. It had a plump lounge and a well-stocked bar, which Jude was at, downing a shot of vodka as Paloma and George came below deck.

He smiled widely, 'Don't tell Mum.'

'Okay, but no more,' Paloma said, hugging his long, thin body.

'Alright, alright,' he squirmed out of her arms after accepting a kiss on the cheek with a smile and a good portion of hair in his eyes.

'You could live in here,' George said, taking there interior of the yacht in.

'That's a good idea actually,' Jude said, then yelled, 'Mum! Can I live on *Chakra*?'

'No!' came a yelled reply from above.

'Well I tried,' he said, and put his long legs up on the coffee table, which grew on a stem out of the floor like a very expensive mushroom.

'You nearing the end of high school?' asked George.

'Oh God. Not the what-are-you-going-to-do-after-school talks.' He groaned.

'Don't be rude,' said Paloma.

'I get it from Mum and Dad *constantly*. As if I know.

All I know is I don't want to join the family business.'

'Travel?'

'Maybe. What did you do after high school anyway?'

'I barely went to high school. Never graduated,' George said. 'And now look at me.'

'See that Aunty Paloma? He never even finished school. And he's doing okay. He was a pro-surfer.'

'I'm definitely not a role model for anyone. I'd advise against doing any of the dumb shit I've done.'

'I guess I'll do my own dumb shit instead.'

'A solid life plan,' said Paloma.

'You ready or what?' Celine called from above.

Celine pulled a wetsuit over her bronzed shoulders and George was surprised that she was wearing makeup to go diving.

They slid snorkels over their eyes and slipped into the sea. Everything felt quiet and clear. It was almost unnaturally turquoise, fuzzing into the distance. With large mossy rocks and rosettes of an almost fluorescent-green coral blooming underneath them, flashes of their yellow flippers disturbing the tranquillity of the surface.

The bottom of the ocean was dotted with abstract shapes, some soft, some hard, some spongy, and small tips of a violet flower danced: as George moved for a closer look it closed up suddenly, surprising him — where they creatures, or flowers? Or both?

Little striped fish darted in the meaty grasses, fins waving. Everywhere was alive. The green-blue map of algae and coral was teeming.

He felt a spree of unrestrained joy watching the scatter twist of small creatures in the underbrush, many-legged and merry-wriggling.

As they swam along he saw movement ahead — a shape that came into focus as a slow swimming turtle, resembling a sentient rock, moving along the ocean floor, fins moving in slow motion, not raising a bubble.

Spiky coral was haunted with ghost-like fish, almost transparent, above them the sun glittered rippling.

It was mesmerising, almost psychedelic: like being a visitor to another world, an ocean that was very different from the one he knew —the one of swells and sets, of sea storms, of the fast and hard physicality of the surface. How infinite, how spectacularly unknowable it was, how deep, and deeply weird.

Celine and Jude swam ahead of him, slick and fast in neoprene; black seals. Where was Paloma? George looked around. He couldn't see her.

And then he noticed it. A dark, large shape he took for another turtle at first. As it got closer, he saw a rounded pushing face in the light, and he knew it was a shark. It nosed along ahead, nearer Celine, moving with an almost mechanical motion. He felt a moment of pure panic, watched as the shark, uninterested, moved past Celine and Jude slowly and then back into the distance, its tail rhythmically moving from side to side as it vanished.

Celine turned and motioned to George to return to the boat. He didn't need the instruction.

Back on the surface George shook. Jude laughed, nervously, pushing his wet hair back.

'Some trip, huh?' Celine said, eyes widening.

'That was amazing,' George said. 'Remind me never to do it again.'

'Paloma!' Jude called. 'You didn't dive? You just missed the most crazy thing . . .'

The rest of the day was calm and light. Paloma and George warmed in the sun, salty-limbed, ate, drank, talked, didn't talk. Was this what her entire life was like? Is this how the wealthy spent their time? The slow sensuality of sun and sea took the burn out of George's thoughts, and he felt dazzled and delighted with the festive air of just being there with her.

———

George was never really sure which he leaned towards more: poetics or protocol. He loved the nebulous, the mysterious, things lightly named and deeply felt. Yes. But he also needed order. He needed to believe that everything had a place, a reason. This he strove to believe, sometimes contrary to lived experience. He could study the waves, the laws of meteorology, of nature, even feel spiritually connected to the processes bigger than himself. He felt he could, in part at least, predict things. Yet it was senseless, too. Waves and weather were sometimes unpredictable. Was that part of the thrill? Having his deep need for order constantly upended?

He saw much in his life as a PI that didn't make

sense. It felt like his own small act of justice, of reason in reasonlessness, to make a kind of order out of things, to quest for the truth as much as a man could.

George talked under his breath softly, walking the length of the beach, thinking.

A figure approached him from the other end of the beach, a familiar figure in a Missoni bikini, a nest of warm hair.

'Want some company?' Iris asked as she neared.

'Sure.'

They walked together. Her slender feet made almost no indent in the firm sand.

'Tell me to mind my own business,' she said into the warm wind, 'but were you and Paloma a thing?'

'A thing? Oh yes.'

'She doesn't let much slip,' said Iris. 'Women's intuition.

'So,' she continued, '*were* or *are*?'

'Past tense, I'm afraid.'

Iris watched him, amused. 'Still carrying that torch huh?'

He smiled sadly, shrugged.

'Lucky her.' She had delicate little teeth in her smile. It reminded George of a woodland critter, ready to tear into a nut.

'I was going to ask you out for a drink,' she said. 'But now I won't. I guess.'

She smiled at him again, looked him up and down. 'Too bad.' She walked into the ocean, with a quick smiling look back at him, before diving in.

—

A missing husband could be a welcome turn of events for some wives. Was Iris one of them? George found her basic info easily enough, date of birth, marriage record, previous address in South Yarra. She'd been employed at a university for the last six years. Had married an Andrew Quade, kept her name, shared her bank account, spent five years with the man before he went missing.

Andrew was more interesting, the records painting a picture of a thorough deadbeat. Juvenile record extended to an adult acquittal for fraud, a few summary offences. What was Iris doing with — and how had she met — a guy like that? George pulled missing persons for Melbourne, looking for Quade. Nothing. Did Iris keep his disappearance to herself, did she have reasons of her own for not contacting the police? What about his family? Maybe she was pleased he'd taken off, happy to have him out of her life for good? There was more to the whole business, and he'd keep looking for it.

George typed up his report and time keeping for Paloma, orderly as any other job. They hadn't even discussed payment, billable hours — the one time in his career George hadn't done so. He knew he should keep things as professional as he could, but he couldn't bring himself to do it. He was all in, regardless.

—

The night felt good as his tanned thighs slipped between crisp white sheets, and he knew it would end soon, that this wasn't real life, as he fell into a cool and deep sleep.

George woke with a jerk, heart-rate climbing, chest slick with sweat. He couldn't tell what had woken him, got up silently, and in the dark felt his way to the door, listening. The house spoke a foreign language; he didn't know its night noises.

He waited by the door — seconds, minutes? — making an inventory of his bodily sensations as a way to create calm and instil patience . . . Feet, slightly tingling, hard on the cold floor. Ankles, tense, tight. Calves, taut, the straining waking his muscles. The impenetrable dark of the house emerged with his growing pupils into a shadowy purple, until he heard faint creaks that seemed out of place, like a light in the dark. He was now alert as the voice of the house spoke to him, with its creaks and hum of appliances, the slow beat of ceiling fans. He padded out, pushed his hands onto the stair rail and looked down. Nothing, which turned into a flash of red as someone moved — fast — down the hall, then nothing again.

Just someone getting up in the night. *Go back to bed.* He looked at his phone, 2.37 am, back in the sheets, awake. Wide-eyed now. Swaddled up in sheets and drifting, he heard a violent crash, then a woman's shriek cutting through the night. He rushed out into the hallway. A man's voice, a woman's. Downstairs a bedroom light was spilling out and Iris stood in her short peach pyjamas, crying.

'What's happened?' George asked.

'I could have *been killed,*' she was saying, choking,

'Oh my God.' George held her, she was clearly in shock.

'Are you okay? Iris?'

'My ankle,' she said, and sank to the floor.

George looked at it: it was red and grazed, puffing already.

The noise had brought out Celine and Walt. 'I'll get some ice,' Celine said quickly, mum-mode activated.

'No! What if they're still here?' Iris shrieked.

'Try to be calm,' said Walt, in a thick navy-blue robe with neat hair as if he were waiting on set for his next scene. 'What happened?'

Iris looked confused, her pointed-nail hands shaking.

'I . . . I was going to get a glass of water, still half asleep. I saw the light on in the study, heard someone in there, but didn't think anything of it. I mean we have a teenager up all hours. It all happened so suddenly, I didn't have time to realise what was happening — I suddenly felt someone push me down the stairs *hard!* I don't know how, I somehow managed to hang on to the rail. I was clinging for my *life!* I've hurt my ankle, and my hip feels weird,' she said, looking down to a ballooning pink foot, now resting on a pillow Celine had brought.

'Did you see anything?' asked Walt.

'It was so dark, I was still half asleep. I did see a bright colour, red or pink maybe. I don't know!' She stared at her feet, gasping.

'We need to search the grounds now while there's still a chance someone could be out there,' George said. Iris grabbed his hand and pulled him close. 'Don't leave me!'

'It's okay, I'll stay with you.' said Celine, who was examining Iris's ankle. 'Let's get you on your bed and I'll wrap this up.'

'We'll go check it out,' George said, motioning to Walt. 'I doubt anyone would still be here but we'll make sure.'

Walt switched on the outside floodlights. 'You take the front drive,' he said to George. 'I'll go left, we'll meet at the back door.'

'Wait, is the alarm on?' George asked.

Walt checked. 'No. And the front door is unlocked.'

'Call out if you notice *anything*,' George said, and they went on their separate paths into the crisp night.

He walked down towards the gates, senses sharp. Nothing but frosted stars and long-shadowed trees. The further he walked from the flood-lit house, the more nervous he felt. He slipped across the grounds quick as a cat.

He shook the front gates, secure. Beyond, the thump of the sea and the night.

Once he was back inside, he found Iris was calmer, her ankle wrapped and iced. Celine said she'd sleep the rest of the night in Iris's room.

'The study is a mess. Looks like it's been ransacked,' Walt said to George. 'I'll do a proper inventory for insurance, but I think we were lucky, that's the only room that looks disturbed and there's not much there to take really. Who knows why they'd target it. I'll let island security know, and then let's go back to bed.'

———

The study felt like a gentleman's club from the 1930s: red-leather chesterfields, book-lined walls, tobacco-stained oil paintings, an imposing mahogany desk, glinting curios. The walls were deep red damask, the curtains heavy, brass gleamed dully, Chinese satin cushions sat on the chairs.

The only points of light came from bottle-green banker lights and slits of sun from the heavy sashed windows.

The place was usually orderly, even immaculate. Today, the thick-piled carpets were covered with papers and objects.

George picked up a polished oak, nautical-style clock from the floor. Behind glass marbled with cracks it read 2.36 am. He darted from the floor back to the desk, over to the window and back again, lips moving with inaudible questions.

'You need any help in here?' Paloma startled him.

'How long were you standing there?' he said, self-conscious.

'Practically hours.'

'Well, come on in then and help, instead of being a voyeur. Have a good look around. If you notice anything missing, let me know. I've already got a list from Walt; a laptop's gone, a camera, some valuable candlesticks, because that's a real thing that people own, apparently.'

Paloma looked around the room, tidying as she went.

'Whose laptop was it in here?' asked George.

'It's Dad's old office. No one else uses this room or anything in it, as far as I know, so I guess it's Dad's. Not that I've ever looked at it. Couldn't bear it.'

'He kept paper records here as well?'

'I guess so.'

'Oh!' said Paloma, 'this is weird, but have you seen an ivory letter opener? I used it yesterday and then put it back on the desk.'

'A letter opener? Doesn't seem likely to be something people would steal,' he said.

'I'm not saying it isn't weird. Is it here?'

'Not that I've seen. Okay, so, a laptop, a camera, some candlesticks, an ivory letter opener . . .'

'You're saying it was an unhinged person. That's comforting.' She went to a safe, swung it open.

'The safe,' she said, 'It's open.'

She looked through.

'What was in here, do you know?'

'Dad's gun and some personal papers, maybe some jewels of Mum's but I'm not sure. Everything is gone.'

—

George wore a sheet of sweat, lying in the crisp white bed, the fan fluttering above rhythmically. He got out his phone. Nothing. Made a new note:

Old Mate's laptop —Syd office?

Security cam?

A — deep background

Gun?

No time like the present.

He called a familiar number. A brisk female voice answered.

'You've got Mallory.'

'George Green here. How you been?'

'Georgie! Long time, no see. Same same. Y'know. What do you need?'

'Detailed background. Guy's showing up clean for me, but my gut says no.'

'What are you looking at him for?'

'Not sure yet. Maybe blackmail. Maybe not.'

'You   got   a   visual?'

'Yep,' he said, looking at the photo Paloma had texted to him when he'd requested it earlier. 'Emailing it to you right now. Name and DOB in the email.'

'Righto. Just checking my email, hang on. Hel-*lo*, that's the best smoulder I've seen in a long while, bar yours of course. You've seen what the boys in the office look like so you know I appreciate it.'

'Thanks Mal,'

'Anytime. Well, anytime I don't have anything better on.'

'Love your work,'

'Yeah, yeah.'

6.

Yes, she was dying, but Paloma was feeling kind of great. Everything familiar had taken on a rosy hue, as if the stars in the sky were addressing their beauty specifically to her.

She'd slept well, despite the break-in the night before, and had woken feeling unaccountably happy for the first time in a long, long while, lying under the slowly turning ceiling fan as the morning light strayed across her bed.

A flutter of white by the door caught her attention: a scrap of paper on the floorboards, gently lifting in the fan's breath. It hadn't been there when she went to bed, she was sure of it. She left the cloud of her bed, barefoot, and picked it up slowly.

It was a print out. It read:

Are you doing anything yet? You'd better start listening to me.

Phoebe Harris.
Gregg Coleman.
Sean Longworth.

Paloma opened her door and looked down the stairs: there was no one.

What next? She laughed to herself at the absurdity of the situation. Anonymous letters. Notes under doors! It scared her that this had been slipped casually under her door; that the person, whoever it was, had access to the house. That it could be one of the family, or the numerous staff, or yes, the thief from previous night. *You'd better believe I'm googling these names,* she thought.

Phoebe Harris: a NZ swimmer, a beauty queen, a woman executed for 'coining' in 1786, a UK 'adventurer' on Instagram . . . who had spent some time on Songbird Island a while back, according to her photos. Paloma studied her face, but she didn't look familiar.

Neither of the other two looked familiar to her either, but one of the Greggs had spent some time on Songbird Island, according to his photo feed. As Paloma scrolled a Gregg Coleman's Instagram she saw a series of familiar views, most dated 2016. What did it mean?

George might have an idea. He'd certainly have those arms of his — and she wanted to see them, *So help me.* She put on a long, thin-strapped white dress, and left her room to find him in his own.

'Let's go for a walk,' she said, and he jumped up from where he'd been sitting on the bed on his phone, eager as a golden retriever.

They walked out, bare feet on the well-kept track from the house to the private beach, faces stroked every now and then with abundant glossy leaves.

'So what do you think it means?' she asked.

'Maybe nothing. Maybe something. I'll look into it. The more interesting thing at this point is the fact that this was slipped under your door. The other letter at least attempted to hide the sender's proximity. This must've been someone who can get into the house easily and not arouse suspicion. How many staff are here in the house?'

'Um, a couple of cooks and cleaners, I don't know who else. That's Cee's thing.'

'Will you get me a list?'

'Okay,' Paloma said.

As they reached the beach they had run out of official conversation. Gazing at him, Paloma tried to decide whether she wanted to really talk to George, to know what he'd been doing since she'd left, whether she really wanted to know the answers. She knew that part of her still wanted him to say *I messed everything up with you. After you my life fell to pieces. I haven't been the same.* A part of her that she was not proud of wanted him to be a failure without her. She was surprised that this part of her existed, even now.

'Anyway. Let's talk about something that isn't,' she gestured broadly, 'all that. Tell me what you've been doing with your life.'

George returned her gaze, hair gently blowing into his eyes. 'It's not much of a story.'

'That's evasive.'

He shrugged. 'What about you? What have you been doing with your life?'

'Oh mine's too sad a story and I'm too sad to tell it,'

she said, looking out to the glassy turquoise sea. 'Tell me about your adventures. Why'd you quit surfing?'

He looked bemused. 'Okay. Surfing,' he kicked the sand. 'Ultimately I think it is better just to do it for fun and my own thrills. Not for money or competition or any of that. It was fun at first, and then unbearably . . . I don't even know. I wasn't impressed by it anymore. I needed something else. So I left.'

'And became a private investigator. Though in a way I'm not at all surprised. Remember when we first met? Or that time you saw a drug bust going down in that park in Sydney, undercover cops and everything and I hadn't noticed a thing?' She laughed.

'I do,' he smiled. 'You were always too busy seeing the good in everything to notice the grime.'

'So a PI. Why not a cop?'

'Can you imagine me being told what to do? I'm too fuckin' old to change my ways. I think I just wanted to help people, to get out of own head for a bit. It made sense at the time. I suit it anyhow.'

'Do you? Help people?'

'Not as often as I'd like. Little victories are still victories.'

They scrambled over rocks as they headed further down the stretch of beach to the public area, solitude giving way to the gentle presence of tourists.

'You still in that same place in Bronte?' Paloma asked, attempting to sound light, though she had so many memories attached to the house, a different version of herself sitting at its kitchen table, lounging in its bed, reading in its back garden.

'I probably will be forever,' he said. 'You ever planning on going back to Sydney?'

'I'm not really planning anything for the future right now'.

'Why not?'

'I just want to get through the present. That's enough some days. Some years. Just get through them.' She felt self-conscious suddenly, and pushed her hair back from her face.

'But it's a human necessity, isn't it, having something to look forward to?'

Paloma turned her eyes, and the question, back to George 'What are you looking forward to?'

'Sleeping under the stars. I've got a trip lined up next year, down south. That place we . . .' he too looked uncomfortable suddenly, wondering if she knew the one he was talking about. She knew.

'Anyway,' he said quickly, picking up a rock, skimming it. 'It's good, it's natural, to be excited about something, anything, in your the future. Getting a new place. Going somewhere different. Having a kid. Getting a dog. Whatever.'

'I guess you're right.'

'That'd be new.'

———

Later, Paloma thought about what he'd said. What *was* she looking forward to? How long had it been since she was excited about the future? Why hadn't she made any plans past being here? Was she ready to just give up? What would it matter if she did? If she just died, here, now?

It was nice that Cee didn't question her. Cee liked having Paloma around, so she didn't push, didn't ask. Paloma's life had settled into a routine: swim, eat, read, hang out, drink, sleep, repeat. She had considered it was all part of her grieving process. How long could she truly spend, being idle, here on the island? Why did anything else make her feel heavy as a planet?

Death had split her life into before/after. She'd never dealt with grief before, not of her own.

A while after her dad died, she had booked into a hotel in Sydney. The idea of being in her own house was unbearable. She didn't want to take calls or emails about work — couldn't imagine going on a shoot again. The idea of anyone seeing her made her feel as if her face would crack; her ribs would split open and offer up her viscera.

Hotels had always had a certain appeal: they were insulation. The rest of the world, time, maybe evolution itself, no longer existed once you were inside a hotel's anonymous walls. The smooth rules of hotel life, hotel portions, hotel pleasures, dimly lit bars serving overpriced cocktails to overenthusiastic tourists, buffet breakfasts and pillow menus, consistency.

She found a hotel online that appealed — grey concrete and plush velvet and bursts of pampas grass — and booked it for two weeks without consciously registering the price. She checked in and in her suite she pumped the AC to seventeen degrees, showered with herbal toiletries, poured a gin and soda, and then hid, naked, under the plump quilt. She slept. She finally relaxed.

Day after day, tray after tray of room service. She watched *The Long Goodbye* and *Bill and Ted's Excellent Adventure*. She watched *Call Me By Your Name* and *La Collectionneuse*. She watched most of *Lodge 49*. She took long steamy baths in the huge marble tub and watched the people at the bus stop below, making up little stories about their lives, where they were going and with whom. She ordered more bottles when the mini bar faced drought.

In the morning — was it morning? Probably afternoon, she made coffee in her room. She read random books on her Kindle, unable to concentrate for more than a few pages at a time. In the mornings — probably afternoons — she read the papers she had ordered the night before. Paloma hadn't read newspapers before, yet now found that she liked their tactility, the smell of newsprint and the orderliness of their columns. She'd do the crosswords.

Sometimes she'd turn her phone on. Usually Celine, usually concerned. Celine was busy enough and with enough of her own life that she wasn't overly, or intrusively, concerned.

Messages from friends. From KJ. *Just checking in.* So polite they didn't make any sense. There was nothing polite about any of this. They were good-hearted, Paloma could see that, so she'd reply with something short, never something heartfelt, because what could her heart say that was true? What her heart felt couldn't be put into words, or not into short and comforting words, telling people they didn't need to worry. Telling KJ she just needed some time on her own. She put her ear to her hotel room wall and strained to listen for signs of life in other rooms.

———

'Are you sick?' the taxi driver had frowned. The scrubby ribbon of the median strip on the highway rushed past the car and Paloma did, in fact, feel extremely nauseous. His eyes were worried.

'It's okay,' she said with glassy eyes, 'I won't throw up in the car.'

She had finally decided to check out of the hotel after talking to Celine.

'Where the fuck *are* you?' Celine had asked over FaceTime, no longer unconcerned.

'Some hotel,' Paloma said in her white robe, wondering idly how long she'd been at the hotel. Ten days? Eleven?

'I'm booking you a ticket to come home tomorrow,' she had said. So that was that.

So Paloma cleaned up, got dressed, paid her room service bill. Paloma went back to her blinded apartment, dark and sour with being closed in, somehow not hers anymore, like it had rejected her, as if someone else had been living there. Whoever it was hadn't watered her plants.

She packed a suitcase.

She held it together on the taxi ride, but when the driver, with some relief, handed her the suitcase, it felt as if it were full of heavy metal, pots and pans and cast iron skillets, it was all unbearably burdensome, and as he drove away she threw up in the gutter outside the airport.

Then she went inside like nothing had happened and ordered a full breakfast, and went back home.

—

They'd given him twelve months, he lasted five. Five! she protested to herself. Paloma held his hand while he was alive, and then when he was dead. Barely changed, entirely different.

Home.

The idleness, the sun, the enveloping heat, the slow-moving ocean, the lack of responsibility, it made Paloma feel she was floating.

She was actually feeling a bit better, as she sat on the beach, beer in hand, bare feet and knowing Celine and Walt and Jude, and even Iris, were up there in the house, living their lives. Getting on with things.

Just like that, her heart began to beat against her chest as if she'd just run a few kilometres. She was dizzy. The sky turned upside down — how dare it. She felt adrenalin surge, her breath jarring, and found herself unable to move, except to lie back in the sand and think *so this is how I die*. Her breath came in gasps, her heart beat all she could hear, she could feel the blood rush and pump into her brain, feel the streak of it in her temples, the tender tips of her fingers. She trembled violently and dripped sweat.

She couldn't do anything except lie there and accept it. Death on the beach — it sounded like an Agatha Christie novel. Could be worse.

But after a few minutes, her heart began to settle back into regularity, the sky was in its regular place above her, her breath eased and she hadn't died. In fact, she felt perfectly okay, if a little shaky. It almost felt like it had never happened. She'd felt this way back in Sydney, several times, before she went to see a therapist — a woman recommended by a friend as very calm, very good, very expensive. Had it helped? Maybe. The tranquillisers more so.

Later, back in her room, she googled, not for the first time:

Why do I feel afraid for no reason?

The sense of dread — about nothing, about everything — stayed with her, close as a familiar darting around her ankles. Sometimes it manifested as particular caution, often to do with food. She could choke on chicken bones. She could get salmonella poisoning. Was the meat cooked properly? She checked and re-checked expiry dates. Threw out whole meals, scraping them into the bin quickly, hiding them with paper towels. She never ordered meat when she ate out, too risky. She counted down the minutes after she ate, wondering when the pains of food poisoning would hit. She knew that she was acting irrationally, yet she did it nonetheless.

She was marching towards her own execution,

death everywhere. She worried endlessly about Celine and Jude. Her thoughts would run on and on in spirals.

She saw it for what it was, yet she couldn't stop. She hid it as best she could, and no one, blessedly or cursedly, seemed to notice, aside from her therapist.

The panic attacks got easier in a way, because by the time she was back on the island, she knew them for what they were. They came, they passed.

She'd grown used to her new companion, and after another few sessions of therapy on FaceTime realised that she wasn't dying, as much as her mind tried to convince her otherwise. She clung to good thoughts like a wildflower on a cliff face. Paloma had read all she could about anxiety and panic attacks, talked at length with her therapist, and realised she needed to make friends with her shadows. Ignoring them wasn't working. Annihilating them felt wrong. So she had another way forward that she could see: she could understand them, and treat them with kindness. She wanted to know: When the heart's pieces came apart, how did it heal again? Could it?

7.

Paloma took his photograph. He had been used to it when they were together — the ever-present camera, her third eye, she would take it out whenever something spoke to her. Often he was lucky enough that it was him. This was the first time she'd taken his photo in — God knows how long — and he wondered what she had seen. What she saw when she looked at him now.

It was golden hour on the beach, the light falling across Paloma's skin in broad gold streaks, turning her black eyes a dark, rich amber. They were doing nothing except being present for the beauty of it, talking idly into the warm breeze, when she turned her camera towards him. He felt energised by her attention.

She looked quietly at her viewfinder and then back up at him, smiling.

'Cee and the rest of them are down at the bar. You feel like going for a drink?'

'I really do,' he said.

The evening fell softly around them as they walked quietly, just like old times, bare-legged. He remembered summers; hands tracing Paloma's bare skin, running them over the white scar on her head *I got it when I was a baby*, joining the freckles on her back and naming the constellations:

A pear.

Twelve o'clock.

Paraguay.

She was wearing lipstick the colour of theatre curtains and her jewellery glinted like footlights.

The bar was all warm wood and deep pools of light, dimly lit bottles glowing like an apothecary, the sweeping vista viewed from an expansive outdoor deck.

They got drinks — George a beer and Paloma a negroni — and went out onto the deck. Celine, Iris, Walt and Adam were at a booth. Iris hugged Paloma and then George enthusiastically, 'Hi handsome.'

'Sit,' Celine motioned to George, with an amused glance at Iris, and leaned in to talk. 'How are you liking being here on our island?' she stirred her drink.

'It's beautiful.'

'And how do you like seeing Paloma?'

'She's something to see.'

Celine smiled. 'So what does a detective do exactly, if you don't mind me asking,' she said, *sotto voce*.

'How would I know?' George replied innocently.

'Oh don't worry. Your secret's safe with me. You know how it is with sisters,' she said.

'Well, y'know. The usual.'

'No I *don't* know. Like, cheating husbands?'

'And wives. Missing persons. Some corporate stuff.'

'And you're good at it?'

'I don't like having a boss,' he shrugged. 'It works out.'

'I suppose you've seen some things . . .' led Celine.

'You wouldn't believe it.'

'Maybe I would.' she said. 'What about blackmail?'

'I'm against it.'

'You're cute,' she said. 'You won't give a thing away.'

'The word "private" is in the job title.'

As they talked, a guy squeezed onto the end of the booth next to George and Celine.

'Hello,' he said to Celine, ignoring George, 'I couldn't help noticing that you're the most beautiful woman in this establishment, and I thought to myself, "I need to talk to her or spend the rest of my life regretting it."'

'Well now you're talking, what did you want to say?' Celine said smoothly.

'How old are you? If you don't mind me asking.'

'How old are you? That's what you settled on?' She laughed. 'Oh, I've been around a while now. I'm turning forty in a few months, if it comes down to actual numbers.'

'Forty!' The guy whistled, 'Hey guys —' he turned around to a group of men standing at a nearby table, 'she's forty!' in amazement, then back to Celine. 'If you look this good now, I can't imagine how hot you were at twenty-three.'

'I'm not sure that works as a compliment,' Celine replied, still amused. 'I'm guessing you're twenty-three then? At your peak?'

'Don't hold it against me,' he said. 'I'm Noah,' and leaned over George to shake her hand.

'Celine.'

'I'm George.'

'Oh shit, you guys aren't together or anything are you? You don't look like you are. No offence mate,' Noah said.

'None taken.'

'No, that one over there is my husband,' Celine said, pointing to where Walt was talking to Iris and Paloma.

'Lucky man,' Noah replied, 'but if you'd prefer to go home with someone else tonight, I'm *definitely* here for you, beautiful,' and returned to his mates with one last appreciative look.

'Glad Walt didn't see that,' Celine said. 'Where were we?'

Where they were was forgotten: Paloma took Noah's place at the end of the booth.

'So, what do you do when you aren't teaching kids or surfing or solving crimes?' Paloma asked George politely. *Oh don't be polite*, he thought.

'That actually pretty much covers it. I do my washing every now and then, I suppose.'

'Glamorous,' laughed Celine.

'You like teaching?'

'I do. They don't listen to a thing I say for the most part, makes me proud.'

'I have a kid. I get it. What do you charge?' asked Celine. 'Jude'd like a few private lessons next time we're in Sydney.'

'I don't do it for money.'

'Only love?'

'I do everything for love,' George said.

Adam slunk over. Shirt buttons, if he even had any, entirely unused.

'Celine,' he said, sibilant voice floating off with fumes of booze. 'I have a proposition for you.' He motioned for her to join him.

'Sounds delicious,' she squeezed her way out, a waft of dark perfume in her wake.

'What's Adam's deal anyway?' George asked, watching them talk closely.

'Interesting, in a nebulous sort of way, though I can never put my finger on exactly why. Not what I'd call easy-going. I don't think anyone could genuinely connect with him unless they shared his primary interest.'

'Which is?'

'Money. Sex maybe a distant second? Why he gets along with Walt so well I guess.'

'So there's nothing between you two?' George said.

'What? He is not at all my type,' she said. 'I haven't changed *that* much. Why, are you jealous?'

'You'd better believe it.'

Paloma smiled.

'You think he's above board?' he continued.

'I suppose so. I mean, I give everyone the benefit of the doubt until proven otherwise.'

'That's what's lovely about you.'

'Just that?'

'Well, no, but if I start a list I'll just depress myself.'

The energy in the room swelled and quickened and a tray of shots appeared.

'Get 'em in,' said Adam. Celine gently poured a shot into George's mouth.

Just what I don't need, he thought, remembering the forgetting of past tequila nights.

The night burned on, the sea deep blue, then inky, then invisible, except for a dark incantation below the deck. The bar filled, post-dinner guests added to the convivial air, music getting louder, people looser.

George was at the bar.

'This place is full of pussies,' Noah said to him, 'I'm going to start a fight with every single man in this bar.'

'Fair enough,' said George. 'One quick favour, can you start from the other end?'

'Jesus,' said Noah, 'you're all right.'

The younger man was animated, sloshing his beer near his lips, half the mouthful absorbed into his dark beard.

'You take it easy,' George warned, and decided to keep his eye on him.

—

Iris was in a bathroom stall, issuing helpless tremors of laughter. Outside the door, George called: 'Iris? Is that you?'

'I just . . .' Iris laughed again. 'Come in,' she said, swinging open the door.

George went in to find Iris pulling her top down, her phone on the toilet lid.

'What are you doing?' George said, laughing.

'The line in the ladies was ridiculous. I just texted someone a nude. I think I sent it to the wrong number, can you check my phone? I hope it was . . . I'm . . . tequila is bad. Awful. Evil.'

George picked up Iris's phone. 'Yep . . . you sent it to Adam.'

It was a while before Iris could talk, clutching her ribs in laughter. 'Oh shit,' she said. She didn't say whether that was the intended recipient.

'C'mon,' George said, organising Iris's top and hair. 'So, you and Adam?' He asked as they left the stall.

'He's a bit of fun,' Iris said. 'Any action with you and Paloma?'

'Still nothing to confess, sadly,' he said.

Iris laughed and then swayed dramatically.

'Let's get you home.'

As they left the bathroom Adam appeared, and said 'Iris, you okay there? I'm heading back, you want me to take you home? You stay George. I got this.'

George watched from the balcony as Iris and Adam left the bar. Clearly having an argument, Adam was gesturing angrily and Iris laughing. Adam grabbed her arm and they walked away.

———

It was loud and light was swimming. Noah approached Celine again, more determined now, definitely more drunk, and ran his hand over her back as he spoke, to Celine's immediate displeasure. She moved away.

Walt appeared — where had he come from, George wondered — and dragged the other man immediately to the front exit.

'Walt!' Celine called. George quickly followed. 'Not you too?' said Celine.

'I'll just make sure nothing happens,' George said.

The next time George saw Noah he was attempting to punch Walt in the face.

Walt stepped into it, so it met him on the shoulder instead, and then he cracked his opponent in the ribs. Noah's breathed a violent HUH as his friends came out of the bar.

George pulled one of them back by the shirt, another of them jumped up and put his arm around Walt's neck from behind.

Not great odds, George thought. But Walt was big and capable, George was slim but physically fit — and despite a spiritual inclination for non-violence, somewhat practised at actual violence.

It was doggish. Noah was not backing down, yelling and darting, and his friends were ready to join in. A crowd gathered. George took a few hits as he tried to get between them and Walt, and he was worried about the looseness of Noah.

'This a private fight or can anyone join in?' A stranger approached George and said, 'What side am I on?' George pointed at one of Noah's mates and the stranger evened the odds.

Walt was focused on Noah, who was definitely not holding his own, throwing wild shots in between taunts. Walt's punches landed. Noah crumpled and Walt, now hot, continued to beat him, holding Noah up to take it, and when he finally crumpled to the ground, Walt kicked him in the ribs.

Security, who knew Walt, had let it run its course until then.

Two of them held back Walt's arms, one said 'That's enough. Let's go inside.'

Walt's eyebrow streamed blood and he was red in the face, but he calmed down quickly, shaking himself out of the brace.

'Alright,' he said.

Inside, the barman poured water for Walt and George.

'What the actual hell do you think you were doing?' said Celine, 'That was savage.'

'Of course it was savage, it was a bloody fist fight,' said Walt. Celine pressed wadded paper towels to his split eyebrow.

'Bit over the top don't you think?'

'There's a reason Aussies fight like hell. Good healthcare and a guarantee no one has a gun,' said Walt and he ordered a round of shots. He seemed carefree for the first time since George had met him.

George had another shot, then there was the vague sensation of walking in the cool night.

'I thought you were a pacifist?' said Paloma, her arm linked through his.

'Well, I'm not Gandhi. Would he be in my line of work do you think?'

'So you like fighting now?'

'Not especially. What was I supposed to do?'

They walked a path back to the house that George wasn't familiar with. He was happy to follow Paloma whatever way she was taking him. Wooden bungalows were quiet, deep in the greenery around them, the sounds of night creatures filling the air. The wind was increasing now, the night sky streaked with the moving squiggles of street-lights. The walk was over before he knew it, suddenly they were home. Paloma unlinked her arm and was gone.

The wind blew, tossing palms like ball gowns. George's room smelled of sea, his head was heavy yet so alert it was almost sickening. He was on the huge white bed trying to cool off under the ceiling fan, he popped two cool white paracetamol, and lay back. The rhythm of the fan cooled his thoughts. His eyes closed.

—

The air was hot and close, the right environment for an orchid, wrong for a hungover man. His voice was raspy. His eye bags had gone from carry-on to check-in.

George felt wilted, sitting on the wide-faced veran-dah trying, failing, to gain reprieve from a blow of sea breeze. Hair of the dog in his hand.

Walt appeared at the open doors, white shirt sleeves rolled up, cool as a marble statue in shadowy museum halls.

'Thanks for your help last night.'

'No problem. You were outnumbered.'

'We were both outnumbered.'

'At least I closed the margin. Made it fairer.'

'Fair. The type of thing you're into, I imagine,' he

said with a smile. 'Being fair. Nothing like a good unfair fight.'

George took a long sip of beer. It was warm as pudding.

'We should go out for a hike while you're here,' said Walt, with finality, and a breezy charm.

'Yeah. Sounds great. Maybe not right now though.'

Walt laughed. Floated off leaving George sick and thick with thoughts.

'You two buddies now or what?' asked Paloma as she came onto the deck.

'He's beautiful, isn't he?' George said.

'I guess. You're not bad yourself. What, is it a friggen beauty contest out here?' she smiled. 'How are you?'

'I'm alright,' he said.

'I know that look,' Paloma said, sitting across from him. 'What's up?'

'I want to talk to you. There are things I've done, things I haven't said, it's been so long that I've wanted to say them.'

'It's okay George, what's past is past. I'm okay. Really.'

'Maybe I'm not. I won't be, until I tell you. Until you forgive me.'

'I have.'

'I haven't, though. I can't move on until I tell you how sorry I am. About it all, how bloody stupid I was.'

'All of it?'

'Well there's a lot I don't regret. I'd never be sorry for us being together. I'm not, I can't explain myself properly right now. Later, when I'm less hung over?'

'Later.'

———

Sullen, unsatisfied, George sought solitude on a smaller, less populated beach away from the house. He felt a growing vulnerability: the kind that made him seek female company, and whatever way he looked at it, it was a bad move. He wanted to take refuge from everything in Paloma's arms.

Instead he bought a Gatorade and hot chips from the takeaway window of the beachside fish'n'chip shop, grabbed a copy of *The Big Sleep* from a bookshelf, a towel, and set himself up in a shadowy spot as far as he could walk without vomiting. Even if he saw a brown snake crawling out from the brush, he thought, he'd be hard-pressed to find the motivation to move.

Watching the ocean was usually easy, but even that was too hard, and George found his eyes taking longer and longer blinks until they closed into sleep.

The sun beat on and on in perfect accord with his head: when he woke, groggy, an apparition in white was in front of him.

'Hello,' Celine said, blocking the sun's rays.

'You look better than I feel,' he said, voice thick. 'What time is it?'

Celine nestled beside him, bare feet curling in the sand.

'Two-ish. Walt's perfectly fine, wouldn't you know

it. Apart from the sexy new cut above his eye. I don't think he even gets hangovers, the bastard.

'The guy, the one he beat up? He's got a broken nose, among other things. Ferried over to the hospital on the mainland this morning.'

George squinted his eyes, looking into the distance, wondering placidly if he was going to throw up. 'Is Walt normally violent?'

'He's not violent, not really. Temperamental. Likes the occasional fist fight. Never, and I mean never, towards me or Jude.'

George's thoughts drifted off with the glittery sea, and they stayed silent for a long while as the day burned on.

'I suppose you get people wanting your help all the time,' Celine said. 'Only, I'm not used to asking for help.'

'You need help?'

'Oh it's nothing, not really . . . I'm being blackmailed.'

George sat up, his stomach curling into folds.

'Who's blackmailing you?'

'Adam.'

'I haven't told anyone this. Not even Paloma, and Paloma and I tell each other everything.'

No, you don't, thought George.

'I've done something potentially very dumb,' said Celine.

'This sounds exciting. How dumb?'

'I can't tell Walt about it. That's the idea. I mean I realised Adam was competitive, ambitious; I didn't realise he was malicious too. If I did, I never would have . . .'

'Why don't you start at the start. This is what I do for a job, I won't judge you.'

Celine smoothed down her billowing dress, adjusted the straps.

'I like men,' she said.

'I bet they meet you halfway,' George replied. It didn't take the smartest PI to figure out both she and Walt were as much extra as marital.

'But I love my husband,' she continued. 'I occasionally see men who aren't my husband. I imagine he sees the occasional woman, too, though he is very discreet. The men, Walt's women, it's only because they're beautiful, or interesting, and it's fun. A diversion. Doesn't that make me sound shallow? I believe in forever relationships, yet I also think a brief, beautiful experience can add something, a different energy, to keep a marriage going. You've got to maintain something secret for yourself, in order to give enough to a relationship like that. For twenty years. Look, I'm not here to justify my actions.'

George wished he had a cigarette. He gulped Gatorade.

'The thing is, Walt would never be able to accept it, not with someone like Adam, not if it were public in any way. I mean just look at what he did to that poor guy who touched me in public last night.

'I don't want a divorce. So, you see my predicament. Not sure if I've ever been in a predicament before. Not sure I'd recommend it, either.'

'How much is he asking? Have you paid him anything yet?'

'A whole lot. We're pretty well off. He knows it, to the dollar. I've paid him once. Now he wants more.'

'Where did the money come from the first time?'

'I have my own account, naturally, but Walt is the one who does the finances, so he'll notice if I withdraw huge chunks of money. I'm just worried at where Adam will stop. If he'll ever stop.'

'Does he have any tangible evidence of the affair?'

'Yes,' said Celine. 'On his phone.'

'Texts from you, that sort of thing?'

'A video. Made without my consent. He belongs in a pond.'

'Do you have any evidence of his demands to you?'

'No. He did it verbally. The personal touch.'

'Our first step is gaining solid evidence that a demand has been made. We need to go through with a payment and gain as much proof as we can, as quietly as we can. Then we can take it to the police,'

'No way. Walt will find out if we go to the police. Can't we keep it between us?'

'There are other options. You could continue to pay him, or . . .'

'Or what?'

'How much do you know about Adam and his past?'

'Well, nothing really. Why? What are you thinking?'

'If he's happy to blackmail you there's a very good chance it's not his first dodgy deal. If we were to find out about something else it may give us some leverage. The preferable option is prosecuting him for that other crime, if there is one, getting him put away so he can't do any more damage. Take the teeth out of his bite.'

'I like the sound of that.'

'How much time do we have? When does he want you to pay by?'

'The end of the week.'

—

George looked at the little slip of paper.

'Okay mate, we're listening to you now,' he said.

Phoebe Harris.

Sean Longworth.

Gregg Coleman.

Who were they? They were clearly connected to this whole saga, whatever it was, but how? It wouldn't hurt to talk to them and find out. Paloma had organised to give him access to the payroll system and HR records online, as quietly as she could.

A good place to start. He'd pull up their records, pay them a little visit, get a handle on their vibes, see how they connected.

Harris, Phoebe. A casual hospitality employee on an NZ Special Category visa, started working on the island seven years back. An unusually long time for a hospo worker to stay in one casual job, though NZ visas were indefinite. She clearly liked it here. Or had other reasons for staying. George glanced at her pay-slips in the system; only had three days off in seven years. Well good for her and her health, he thought. He noted down her details. Like many of the island staff, she was in the official staff accommodation buildings. He called the listed mobile number. No longer connected.

Longworth, Sean. Again, employed for a reasonably long time on the island, five years and counting. UK visa this time. Accommodation on the island. A plumber. He jotted down the particulars, gave the number a call. It rang.

'Hello,'

'Is that Sean Longworth?'

'Who?'

'Sean.'

'Nah mate, no Sean here. Wrong number.'

Coleman, Gregg. Let's see what you've got for us. George noted the details, another long termer, island accommodation, no visa. His number rang out.

George gathered his things, shut down the computer, and decided he'd pay a little visit to the island accommodation, see if he could track any of the trio down directly.

Staff who decided to live on the island were given the option of the reduced-rate employee accommodation. Set deeper into the island, beyond the glittering hotel and views of the ocean-facing windows, the path led George though a maze of semi-detached units with spiky palms, to a multi-storey building beyond. He looked up Phoebe's address, and took a lift to the third floor. Off-duty staff members flapped past in thongs, or looked worse for wear in yesterday's uniforms.

302. Door opened by a banana-blonde with a deep, convincing tan.

'Hey,' she said.

'Hi, I'm looking for Phoebe.'

'I don't know a Phoebe,' the woman said in a German accent.

'I must have my wires crossed, sorry.'

'Maybe she was here before me,' the woman said. 'I've been here two months now, so, you know, staff come and go a lot . . .'

'Thanks,' said George.

Sean was 261. George went down the lift.

The woman who answered his door didn't know a Sean and had been living there for six months or so.

Last stop, Gregg. He went because thoroughness compelled him, though he was beginning to realise what kind of chase he was on.

There was no answer. As he went to leave, a neighbour was coming back to his own apartment.

'You know the guy in this apartment?' He asked.

'Who, Lloyd? Yeah, I know him. You need him for something.'

'Nothing urgent,' said George. 'I'll come back.'

George trekked back to the house, thinking.

In the office again, he logged in, pulled up the payslips of Phoebe, Sean, and Gregg, paying closer attention this time. Payment via EFT: every single transaction was going into the same account.

Yes, he was searching Walt and Celine's room; no, he didn't feel bad about it. He was being thorough — and thoroughness mattered. Celine was being black-mailed, successfully, and he wanted to know what else she was hiding. Because she was hiding something: secrets rarely stopped at just one. They had a way of multiplying.

The family were having dinner at the fancy restaurant up above the resort, so they would be out for at least another hour. George had claimed a stomach ailment after last night's drinking session.

'You okay?' asked Paloma, and he tried to look feeble. 'Yeah, just need to sleep it off.'

Celine's room was huge — they all were — and thick with the smell of a bazaar, of chypre and cinnamon and sandalwood and dried flowers and Turkish coffee. Every surface had objects, layers of postcards and journals with handwritten quotes, vintage silks on the walls, antique mirrors, traditional healing and poetry books. Overwhelming, delightful. He couldn't picture Walt in here at all.

He had to start somewhere. Celine's drawers were surprisingly orderly. Her walk-in wardrobe was packed in shades of peach, ivory, nude, black. She had expensive shoeboxes stacked everywhere. He flittered journal pages. Stalked her walk-in. Examined her ensuite. Nothing.

On the plush rug underneath her bed he could see — yes — one indent, two. The heavy bedside table had been moved, had rested there recently. He pulled the bedside back to position it over the indents once more and felt behind it. Something was taped there — a small gun. He paused for a moment, thinking. There was a — was it? —yes — a voice in the house. *Shit.*

He pushed the table back as quickly as he could, listened, straining, heard footsteps coming up the stairs. He dashed into the bathroom, hiding behind the door.

Celine came into her room, there were sounds of her moving around, then entering the bathroom.

George's whole body was pumping with blood, so loud he wondered if Celine would hear it. He considered his options, plausible stories. Pretend he was just being a total creep? Or make the admission that he was doing due diligence for a new client with a blackmail problem? She wouldn't love it, but she'd understand. He hoped. Or perhaps she'd prefer he was a creep? Could be nice to have something on him, given the circumstances. She opened the bathroom cabinet, he heard rattling of a pill bottle, then her footsteps as she stepped back through the room and down the hall.

—

Tailing Adam wasn't hard. The island was self-contained, in a way that pleased George now, yet made him wonder if he'd get tired of the same thing after a time. He had lived in Bronte for longer than he cared to admit. With Bronte there was always the promise of the city beyond, the rich-city poor-city, with its green space and water and hidden beaches. Here on the island, the measure of life was five or so square kilometres. Was that enough? Even when it was five or so square kilometres of paradise? Would the same view, even if it was the perfect view, get dull and confining day after day?

Adam lived in a bungalow set back from the main family house. George was already running deep background, in the meantime he meant to get more information on the man and his routines. For both sisters.

The initial background check on Adam all came up above board: court records, electoral rolls, employment, credit records, bankruptcy, criminal records, driving records. Straightforward. There was absolutely nothing of note — he'd done his taxes, he'd moved around from Sydney to Melbourne sometime a few years back. The paper trail didn't give much away after that.

Then Mallory called.

'Hey Georgie. So. Your friend, the one with the face? More suss than he looks, turns out.

'Real name is Chris Mosely, DOB ten, two, eighty-four. He's got form. A conviction for embezzlement, also tried for money laundering through online payment systems a few years ago, just to round things out. Skated on it thanks to a technicality. Known associations with some unsavoury types.'

'And other aliases?'

'A few here, Charles Pike, Andrew Quade, Billy Kirketon . . . I'm emailing you the info now.'

———

The first few days and nights tailing Adam were easy enough, but blowouts. It was a small place so running into each other again and again didn't arouse suspicion. Adam had a firm routine: up at 6 am, over to the offices in the main hotel by 8 am, a few tasks during the day that took him across the island, then dinner either at the hotel's restaurant, on the island's main street, or at the house with the family.

The third night was dark early with the kind of blowy rain that moved like a murmuration of birds. George was planted in a spot across from Adam's bungalow, with a thermos of tea, thinking of how beautiful it was, even if the visibility was low, as the rain seeped into his hooded jacket and wet his face, running off of his beard.

A flash of red caught his attention at Adam's door and he watched as Celine, in a billowing kimono, dashed inside. *What are you doing Celine?*

He had asked her to keep him informed about their meetings. This was news to him. He watched, myopic with streaming rain, the warm orange squares of the bungalow's windows burning like twin fires in the wild dark. He waited. For how long? Fifteen, sixteen minutes.

There was a sudden scream and a flash, which he first took to be lightning. He crept in the dark closer to the orange windows, muttering *Fuck, fuck, fuck.*

As he approached the bungalow's porch, three rapid gunshots cracked clear in the stormy night. George ducked automatically and thought he could hear feet running at the back of the residence. He bolted to the front door — locked — and looked in at the window. Celine was sagging, sitting on a chair, and at her feet lay Adam, dark blood pooling around him.

George ran around to the back of the place, aware that he had no weapon. It was spouting rain and blanketed in dark, and the door was wide open. George ran over to Adam: dead. Celine was unconscious; fainted, or injured, but alive, not shot anyplace he could see, tied to a kitchen chair. He untied her, called her name. She murmured hazily, in and out of consciousness.

'Celine! Are you okay?'

'Oh I don't know,' she said, laughed, drifted off again.

'Stay awake! Have you taken anything?'

'I . . . Adam gave me something,' she said thickly, and then she saw Adam at her feet, dead.

'Who shot him?' George asked.

'I don't know . . . didn't see . . .' she said, crying. 'That bastard. I told him, I told him . . . Oh God, the video! You need to get it off of his phone before they find it.'

'We need to get you out of here,' George said. George quickly checked Adam's pockets, tables, surfaces, drawers, for the phone. Nothing.

He picked up Celine, who was now laughing softly, or maybe crying, about as easy to lift as smoke.

'Let's go,' he urged. 'Celine!'

'Where are we going?' she said, then: 'You're tall aren't you?'

'Home.'

—

94

George called the nearest police office, which was on the mainland, as well as island security, telling them what had happened at Adam's bungalow. Well, not everything.

Celine was in bed, still drifting in and out of consciousness. He'd brought her up the wide twirling stairs, as quietly as he could manage, not wanting Paloma, or Walt for that matter, to be alarmed until they needed to be. And he wanted to talk to her — privately — before the medic and the cops arrived.

He gave her water, put a cold flannel on her head, and she was more awake than not.

'George,' she said slowly. 'What happened? Adam?'

'Dead.'

'Oh, my God,' she said shakily.

'Walt!' she whispered, stricken, 'the police . . .'

'It's okay. I took you home first, Walt and the police will come later. I wanted to talk to you before they got here. What were you doing at Adam's?'

'Being blackmailed,' she said. 'Like you said, what else could I do?'

'So you went to see him? Pay him off again?'

'He asked me to go there. I had no choice. I had my phone recording it all.'

'And then what?'

'I don't know,' she said, 'We were talking. He must have put something in my drink. Next thing I knew I was tied up and you were there. Who knows what he was going to do. You think he would have kidnapped me? For ransom? What do we do?'

'Give me your phone. We tell Walt and Paloma and

the police exactly what happened. He asked you there, you came, you were drugged, tied up, someone else came in and shot Adam.'

'But I can't tell Walt. Not about the affair! I won't.'

'Okay so we leave that out for now. It's not a lie. We just won't tell them strictly everything at this moment.'

Celine looked relieved, handed over her phone.

George was not feeling relieved. Could he lie to the police? To Paloma? Wouldn't be the first for either, though he never liked it. Now there was a murder involved, the less Paloma knew the better? The police he felt uneasy about, and was still unsure whether it was a good idea. Celine held his hand gratefully.

'Okay. Get my husband,' she said.

———

The paramedic arrived and Walt looked genuinely distressed at Celine's injury, his glacial cool melting.

George made his way back to Adam's to deal with island security. He still felt uneasy. He didn't like withholding anything. He also knew that by telling them about the blackmail, Celine would be implicated in Adam's murder even more than she was now and George was convinced she was innocent. Paloma would suffer too. No, better to tell them the relevant facts, that he was looking into Adam in relation to the letter, that there was what looked like an attempted kidnapping of Celine, that an unidentified shooter had killed him. George himself was a known factor, he hoped, since he'd worked closely with the police in

Sydney for so long, a registered and above board PI.

Still, before the police arrived, George wanted to look at a few things. The recording on Celine's phone for one, but that would have to wait. He moved fast, tracking back to the scene in the rain.

The bungalow was still dark, now with a nervous-looking security guard out the front.

'George Green,' he said, 'Private investigator. I called it in before, spoke to a Hudson?'

'Head of Security,' said the guard. 'In there now.'

'You mind if I just go in and —'

'Closed scene until the police arrive I'm afraid.'

'I was investigating Adam on behalf of the Knightley family,' George said.

'I'm sure you'll have a lot of relevant information for the police then.'

'It would be helpful to speak to Hudson before they get here.'

'At the risk of repeating myself, no can do mate.'

'I think it should be okay for George to just go in for a quick chat?'

The men turned and saw Paloma approaching, looking determined.

'You okay?' George asked.

'Yeah.' She said, then, to the guard: 'It's not going to hurt to have George talk to Hudson is it?'

The front door opened and a thickly built man in his fifties appeared, looking tired.

'It's alright, let him in.'

George went in, leaving Paloma outside with a quick look.

'Bad business,' Hudson said sadly. 'Never had anything remotely like it here. Your usual drunken assault, a robbery now and then. But this . . .' he looked glad to have company.

'It looks like he had sent a warning letter — not quite a threat, though something like it — to the Knightley family. I wanted to know why.'

'What did you find?'

'Not much. If I could look at his computer, before the police arrive, that might help a lot.'

Hudson looked at George. Probably his worst night on the job, as head of security on one of the most tranquil islands in the world. You don't take on a gig like that because you like action.

'After they take the laptop, which they will take, I won't be able to see it again. This is really my only chance to prove he wrote the letter.'

Hudson looked at George, assessing. 'Alright. Quickly then,' he said.

George opened the laptop and, as suspected, it was password protected. Had to try. No time. He went over to the printer, pressed the menu button, then select — it showed a few file names of recently printed documents stored in the printer's memory. Pressed 'print job' for all three, and prayed silently to gods both new and familiar.

The printer hatched sheet after sheet and George caught them as they fluttered, hands full of paper as the machine stopped printing. He quickly folded the sheets into his jacket pocket.

'Get it?' asked Hudson, looking out of the window.

'I don't know. Thank you.'

Hudson nodded to the door. 'The Knightleys are good people.'

—

Paloma and George cut through the night, back to her room.

'What happened? Cee told us the basics, she's still pretty out of it.'

'I was tailing Adam. Celine arrived, then not long after, there were gunshots. I went inside and she was tied up — it certainly wasn't her doing any of the shooting, unless she's learned to tie herself up convincingly.'

'Of course not. Who then?'

They let the question hang in the air, thinking.

'Why did he tie her up? What was he planning to do?

'Kidnap her for ransom?'

'How did he think he'd ever get away with that, right here? And then why did he write the letter at all? If he *did* write it.'

George spread the print-outs on her bed. They leafed through and spotted those words:

Ms Knightley.

I am not a snitch but I feel I must do as conscience compels me . . .

'That still leaves the question, why?' said Paloma.

'Why would Adam point the finger at Walt? Maybe Adam learned a thing or two being his assistant, and had set Walt up in some way, or just knows something he shouldn't, either way he wanted him out of the picture. In any case I don't think it was conscience that compelled him. Money. Hatred or jealousy, also likely.'

'Do you think there's something about Walt to uncover? Affairs, embezzling, something else?'

'Let's say Walt has been financially irresponsible or stealing or whatever, or had affairs, what then? Would Celine even want to know?'

'I'm not sure she would,' Paloma said slowly. 'But I would.'

'Why?'

'I want the truth. So who killed him? And why? It has to be someone here. One of us. You don't think Walt knew . . . There's something else. I saw him — Adam, meeting Iris in secret. I tailed them. I meant to tell you earlier, they met at the day spa after hours the day you arrived. I don't know why they'd need to keep that secret. They're both single, well, sort of. Could she somehow be involved in this too?'

'I have to get back to the scene. The police will need to talk to me. Keep these safe, I'll have a proper look through the rest later.'

—

George's mind burned through motives, scenarios. It was obvious that the letter was smoke to a fire. And who knew how hot it burned?

The Water Police were the first to arrive and were swarming, the area sectioned off with streaks of yellow tape in the wet night. Curious tourists were already at the perimeter.

George made his way to the entrance and told the officer who he was. After a few introductions he was asked — politely — to stick around nearby until homicide arrived from the mainland. So he waited. George sat on the deck, too wired to look at his phone for more than a few minutes at a time, checking one app, closing it, opening another. The air buzzed around him and he felt nervy, like he needed to be in action, doing something. Anything. It was forty-five minutes deeper into the night when homicide showed, though it felt like a year.

After homicide arrived, they went inside and George waited some more. Soon enough, a woman approached him.

Detective Inspector Lewis calmly introduced herself with a quick handshake. 'You found the victim?'

George nodded. He ran down what had happened as clearly as he was prepared to.

'What were you working on here?'

'Adam wrote a letter to Paloma Knightley, accusing her brother-in-law, his boss Walter Eveleigh, of embezzlement. I was looking into it for her.'

'Any truth to the accusations against Eveleigh?'

'Yet to find out.'

'So the shooting just happened to occur when you were tailing him. A coincidence?'

'Perhaps he'd been alerted somehow to the fact I

was investigating him, was pushed to further action with Celine. Of course that's speculation.'

'In any case, it's relevant. I trust you're not going anywhere for the time being?'

'I guess not.'

'Good. We'll need to talk more. For now I'm going to have to ask that you remain on the island, and cease your investigation. You're friends with the family, not just a paying job?'

'That's correct.'

'Well be their friend. That's the best you can do right now. Got a card? I'll be in touch.'

They swapped cards, and George cleared out.

Walking back to the Knightleys, soaked now, hair sticking to his face, he felt hot and tired and several times thought he saw someone following him in the dark.

—

:Play:

    [close sound of movement and fabric]

    [a knock]

    Adam: Hey babe

    Celine: Are you kidding me? Forget it! In case you didn't notice you're blackmailing me.

    Adam: That doesn't have to be a big deal. Romance and money are two separate things, you know that, we could still have some fun Celine.

    Celine: What do you want? I don't have long.

    Adam: Oh c'mon. We've enjoyed each other's

company. It doesn't have to be like that. Sit down, have a drink. I don't want this to be unpleasant. We have to live with each other after all.

[muffled]

Adam: [unintelligible] . . . right? You won't even miss it! I'm over here with no beautiful wife, no millions of dollars, nothing at all really, help me out a little. It's not personal, our time together has been really special to me.

Celine: This has to stop somewhere. How much to make it stop? For good?

Adam: Same as last time, then we'll see.

Celine: And that will be it? You swear? Not that your word means much at this point.

Adam: I swear, babe. Now loosen up. It doesn't suit you.

[muffled]

Celine: [unintelligible] . . . in your bank account. We have to stop meeting. That's it. Walt will find out and —

Adam: Walt! He'd probably be more pissed about the money than about you.

Celine: You don't know the first thing about him.

Adam: Oh don't I? You'd be surprised. I know more about him, about his secrets, than you might think. Or even know yourself.

Celine: Secrets?

Adam: Have you ever looked into his finances? I don't suppose you care much about the affairs, but you might be surprised just who exactly he fucks around with.

Celine: Sure. Okay.

Adam: All I'm saying, maybe check out your husband's bank account sometime. It might surprise you. And maybe watch who you let under your roof.

Celine: [muffled] . . . do you have any water? [unintelligible] Adam! What . . .

Adam: Just relax, you'll be okay.

[muffled sounds]

[shuffling]

Adam: What are you —

[gunshot]

—

George lay in bed, the image of Adam burning in his thoughts. He was familiar with death, but he'd never gained the level of detachment that he saw in others, they were still just people, gone, and the mystery and the tragedy of that never lessened. To be there, then not there. That was the most mysterious, the most momentous of things, natural as it was — or wasn't, in Adam's case. Yeah he was a lowlife. So what? He was a life.

Sleep would elude him when he was in this mood, he knew from long experience. So he got out of bed, not bothering with getting dressed, quietly padded down the stairs, those endless stairs, and went out the side door and into the garden.

Everything was lit by the moon, crisp-shadowed, still and quiet except for the distant call of night birds and steady hazy murmur of the sea, the stars taking on the glint of knives.

It didn't feel any better. Fresher at least. He felt swallowed whole by the night.

He'd been there a while, trying to meditate, when the kitchen lit up.

He sidled up to the house, slowly, nearing the unshuttered window. He neared the window as close as he could, took a quick look. Iris' hair was dishevelled, her robe grasped around her and her mouth was a tight hyphen. Walt had his back to George. He was talking to her in a hiss George couldn't make out.

'No, it's not,' Iris said loudly, 'and nothing will make it okay. I'm getting out of here and leaving this whole mess behind.'

Walt's voice was measured in reply. 'That will look suspicious.'

'I can't do this anymore. I need to get off this goddamned island and never come back, and that's what I plan to do the second I have my money.'

Walt spoke quietly again, George strained to hear.

'What am I supposed to do with that?' Iris replied, louder now.

'Be quiet,' Walt said.

'I won't. I won't be quiet anymore. You know what I want, and if I don't get it by the end of this week, you know what will happen.'

Walt spoke again, softly.

'I don't care,' Iris replied. 'Simple as that, do what you have to do.'

George strained. He couldn't hear their voices. He dared another glance.

Walt had Iris enfolded in his broad arms, circling

her as she rattled with sobs. Her face reached up to his, kissing him, then he pulled away slowly. She threw his arms off her.

'The end of the week,' she said, face pink with crying, and she left the room.

George silently pulled away from the window and returned to the garden.

———

Bacon helped obliterate thoughts and bad visions. The table was set with a full buffet breakfast: bacon, sausages, eggs, toast, coffee, tea, juice. The house fitted together like a puzzle, and seemed remarkably bright and active, showered and dressed. Just as fresh as George didn't feel after his night.

Walt was sitting reading a paper, drinking black coffee, the headlines loud and thick:

One Person Dead After Shooting on Songbird Island

Cyclone Lucie Bringing Dangerous Winds to the Area

Girl Stable After Jellyfish Sting

'A man, thirty, has been confirmed dead after a shooting last night on Songbird Island, police say,' read Walt out loud.

'Police responded to a call around 11 pm last night.

The victim was shot in the abdomen and pronounced dead at the scene, police reports say. His identity has not been released. Police say no arrests have yet been made in relation to the shooting. In a statement, police ask anyone with information to call their twenty-four-hour tip-line . . .'

Walt slapped down the paper.

'At least they kept us out of it,' he said grimly. 'Money does have that advantage.'

'You paid them off?' asked Paloma.

'Did you think this kind of business would do us any good? As far as I'm concerned, Adam never existed. I don't ever want to speak of him again.'

'That's heartless,' Iris said. She was red-eyed and looked tired.

'After what he did?' Walt looked at Iris with simmering anger.

'I'm not saying it was right. But he didn't hurt anyone.'

'Didn't *hurt* anyone?' Walt stood. 'You've got a unique understanding of the word. He tied my wife up, who knows to what end . . .'

George looked over to Iris and to his surprise her eyes weren't on Walt at all, they were on George. They darted away.

'I'm not hungry,' she said, and looked like she was going to be sick. She pushed her plate away loudly and left.

—

After breakfast, everyone had left the room except George. He stared up at Old Mate; those dark eyes with their humour and wisdom. He realised they were the same as Paloma's.

'What do you think of all this?' he asked softly. If Old Mate had an answer George didn't get to hear it. Iris came back into the room, shutting the door behind her.

'George. Can I tell you something, confidentially?' She lowered her voice and sat close to him, and he noticed she was shaking.

'I'm scared of Walt. I wouldn't be surprised if he . . . well, let's just say I think he's capable of anything.

'It's horrible what happened to Adam. I mean, he didn't deserve to die, did he?' Iris's eyes filled with tears that spilled over her cheeks. 'Maybe it's because I lost my husband, I feel so at a loss to see him just . . . gone like that. It's such a shock. And now there's a murderer loose somewhere on the island.'

'You think Walt had something to do with it? Why?'

'Honestly, I'm not saying that. I don't have any real reason to think so. But what if he turned out to be messing with the books? Taking advantage now Uncle Tom isn't around anymore? Tom had a lot of money you know, and Walt thinks everything is his, he's that kind of man. He left everything to Celine and Paloma and Jude, not Walt. Said so in the will. All Walt has is what he gets at his job at the company, and Tom didn't even promote him to CEO like everyone expected before he died. I think Walt was pissed about that. If they were to get divorced, or if anything happened to Celine, Walt'd have basically nothing of his own. Not compared to all this anyway. And . . . well, he likes women too is what I've heard. Everyone's heard. What if Celine were to find out —' She bit her lip and she left suddenly, not waiting for George to reply.

George was left alone, feeling anxious. She had said everything that was contained in the blackmail letter. He looked up again at Old Mate, and now his eyes seemed to take on a different mood.

8.

He was dead. *Dead.* Paloma hadn't been to a funeral before her dad's — well she had been too young to remember a thing about her mum's, so it was like it had never happened. Now here was a second death in her family within the year. Someone on the island had killed him. And Adam tried to hurt Celine. And he was the one who had written the mysterious letter. Why? What the hell was going on with her family?

Nothing was right. This was her cushion. Her home. Her retreat. Nothing was supposed to alter that reality, eat away at that safety. She felt ill. A headache that came in bursts. She drank a negroni — so what if it's morning, she'd had a shock — and scrolled WebMD.

migraine cluster tension sinus brain aneurysm

She felt glad George was nearby, then wondered, would any of this have happened if he hadn't come? Could Adam have found out about them investigating the letter and been spooked into action? How would he have found out? The only other person who knew was Celine, and she was as likely to tell Adam as Paloma was herself. Wasn't she?

It was messy, and Paloma felt like she was watching it spin out of control. Her head hurt and she paced up and down her room restlessly. *No, no, no,* she thought. Her breath came in gasps and the walls seemed somehow . . . wrong. They turned, spun, and she sank onto the floor, heart pounding. She breathed deeply, trying to regain control.

George was there, 'Pal,' he said, 'are you okay?'

She was shaky, afraid to stand, move, blink.

'No, I'm not.'

He held her there on the floor for a long moment, before she regained enough composure to talk again.

'I felt . . . I'm okay.'

They stood warily, him holding her still, then he took her over to the bed.

'Have some water. Do you feel a bit better?'

Paloma drank thankfully.

'I'm alright. It's not the first time. Though it's the first time when someone's been around. Lucky you.'

'Anxiety attack?' He asked.

She nodded. 'They've been better lately. But now with all this happening, it's just the stress I suppose.'

They sat quietly on her big calm bed, 'Just breathe,' George said every now and then.

Her heart throbbed loud in her ears, she could feel its pulse and eddying swirls, a hot snake in her.

George said 'It's okay,' which made her feel like a patient and she said too quickly,

'I know it's okay. I'm not going to die. Not right now,' and she stood, over it all. Tired with hurt. 'Let's get some fresh air.'

The air was fresh, so fresh it sprinkled their faces with water. The sand was dimpled with drops as they made their way yet again into the sea, warm and waiting.

'The police suggested that I stop my investigation,' George said, as the sea cupped them close, a stand-in for each other's hands.

'They did? And will you?' Though Paloma knew the answer from the look in his eye.

'No, no, I don't believe I will.'

'So what next then?'

'With your permission,' he said softly, 'I'd like a forensic accountant to go into the Songbird Island head office in Sydney as soon as possible and start looking into things.'

'For the embezzlement? Walt? So you believe that?'

'I think it's worth looking into now, don't you?'

'Now someone's dead?' She said, then: 'Adam.'

'Chris Mosely.'

'What?'

'His real name.'

'Christ. Okay, let's do it. Let me know the details and I'll give the CEO a call to let them know what's going on. She can be trusted to keep it quiet, we're practically family. Let me tell her.'

'You find anything in the HR records?'

'Maybe.'

'This is scary,' she said and she remembered that he now knew about her panic attacks. He knew something of the new Paloma. That she'd changed. She wondered what kind of difference it would make.

But he looked at her with such a peaceful longing and regret that she felt her muscles relax into the
water.

That night, sleepless, she thought about that longing
and regret in his face.

He had left. All those years ago. It had taken so
long, so blindly long, for Paloma to realise that they
were living together in body, no longer in spirit. What
was it exactly, that signified his absence? It had been so
many small withdrawals, over such a long time.

She hadn't stopped loving or wanting him. Nothing
had changed for her, she felt unbearably sentimental
about the neat way he folded his shirt over the sofa,
felt the infinite tenderness of living with someone you
loved.

It had been wonderful at first. Then he went on
surfing trips more and more. She was used to that,
never minded it. They got longer, more frequent, and
she spent more nights alone in a month than with him.
When he was there, he didn't want to be there. He
was annoyed at everything: from the birds singing to
taking out the rubbish. Everything pricked him and
he would pick fights, get angry, leave.

She waited, at first. We all have our moons of
discontent. She had hers. So she gave him room to
breathe, to work out whatever was going on. But it just
increased the space between them.

One clear September Sydney morning, she knew he was gone from her — and more — he wanted to be. She hadn't wanted to see that he didn't want to be with her anymore. She had always assumed it was a mood, or a depression, she took it for granted that he still loved her, that he would come back to her when he got his head sorted. Maybe he still loved her, but he didn't want this, her, anymore.

He'd been out most of the night, she didn't know where. She received a text from her friend Emma in the morning:

> Georgie was in fine form last night.
> Where were you???

Paloma's thoughts swam, sitting alone at their kitchen table in the clean sun. What was it? Someone else? She remembered how effortlessly seductive he had been when they'd met, how focused and sensual he was. Up until the last few months, anyway.

How long can you keep two people together when one of them doesn't want to be there? It was unbearable to live with someone who she loved, to see his hands, not touching her. His eyes, not on her. His smile, not for her. He didn't have anything for her any more. They would barely see one another, rarely kiss or touch. Whenever she tried to close the distance he would resist, or get angry. She watched him, beautiful, remote, floating further away.

Had he changed his mind about getting married, realised it was a mistake? Fallen out of love with her?

She couldn't give him any more space than she already had. Nor did she want to. They were together, or they weren't.

She resolved to get to the heart of it, hot and bloody and messy as hearts might be. She couldn't go on like this. She knew that he'd probably just flee, but wasn't that exactly what he was doing now anyway, just in slow motion?

She waited in the sun, at their table, drinking coffee. It went cold.

Eventually he rose, rough-edged; Paloma loved every bit of him and his sleep-rumpled face and she knew she had to do it.

'Good morning,'

He muttered a greeting, poured coffee, then moved to go back to bed.

'George?'

'Yeah?'

'Can you please sit down, I need to talk to you.'

He sat. 'What?'

'Where have you been?'

He bristled, 'I went out. Why? What's the big deal? I can go out can't I?'

'Not just last night. You're gone all the time, George. It hasn't been right with us for months now. You're either away, or not really wanting to be here when you are. What's going on with you? I'm worried.'

'I don't know what you mean,' he said.

'So I'm imagining it?'

'I don't know Paloma. Yes, I've been away. I always go away, it's part of the job description. You knew that when you moved in. It's unfair of you to want me to change now.'

'It feels like you don't want to be here. Be with me. Be present and part of this.'

'I don't know what to tell you,' he sighed. 'I'm right here.'

'Is it another woman?'

'Jesussss.' He stood up. 'I'm not having this conversation with you.'

'Why not? I'm your partner, and I'm telling you that I feel like you don't want to be with me. I feel abandoned.'

'That's your own shit. Don't put it on me.'

'What's happening with you? Maybe I can help,'

'So it's help now? You just accused me of cheating . . . . . .'

'I didn't accuse —'

'Of cheating on you, and now you say there's something wrong with me. Which is it?'

'That's what I want to know. What's going on with you. Why you no longer want this.'

'I do.'

'It doesn't feel like it.'

'I'm not having this conversation. I'm tired. I've got a big meeting this arvo, I've got real life to deal with Paloma. You might want to try it sometime.'

He stood and went back into the bedroom. She heard him bang the wardrobe, and he re-emerged, dressed. He picked his keys up from the table and left the house without another word.

Paloma finally admitted to herself that he had left

her and he would never leave her. So she packed her things, wrote a note, left it on the table:

I loved you so much.

He never called.

9.

George mostly liked the police, understood their professional reticence, their detachment, even if he didn't share it. There were some good cops, some bad; most were a bit of both, like everyone else in this world. He had his favourites. Mallory was no-nonsense, had a heart inside that uniform, and there was something about her gaze, when it turned on you it was like you were everything in the world: the intense focus of a lover or a good detective. He'd asked her out for a drink once — she said no. It had worked out well.

What kind of cop, what kind of human, was Lewis? Homicide was a hungry beast, ate people up, even up here in paradise.

Lewis had called and asked him to come in to the station on the mainland. He'd ferried across, after gathering paper records into a folder of all of his findings so far, leaving out the Cee blackmail info. For now, anyway, it seemed like he'd better keep that to himself, and it was a lie through omission rather than outright.

Now his worries and his lines were clear-cut under

the harsh fluorescent lighting of a private anteroom. He made a witness statement with an officer he hadn't seen before. Waited.

'Water, coffee? It's not great but it's hot,' Lewis said, entering the room and talking without preamble.

'Same has been said about me.'

'What?'

'Sure. Coffee'd be good.'

'Smithy! Coffee and water, Room 1,' she called, and sat across from him. She had a careful air about her, like she filed every bit of paperwork correctly.

'So, Green Investigations,' she said.

'Going on two years now.'

'Tell me about the case you're here on.'

'Paloma's an old friend. She received a letter, anonymous, accusing her brother-in-law of embezzling. She asked me to look into it.'

'You got the letter?' He tapped the folder. 'I've seen the statement. Explain to me what the case was.'

Smithy interrupted them then, with plastic cups of water, paper cups of coffee.

'As I said, it looked like Adam had written the letter, far as I could tell,' said George, taking a gulp of bitter instant coffee.

'Any truth to the claims?'

'Maybe. Maybe not.'

'You investigating that too?'

'Yes. I've got a forensic accountant on it in Sydney. The Sydney police — I'll give you my contact — are across it too.'

'And you were doing surveillance?'

'Basic surveillance to see if I could work out why he'd written he letter, who he was exactly.'

'And then he was shot. While you waited outside.'

'That took me by surprise.'

'Did it?'

'I'm here looking into a letter, I didn't — don't — know what else he was involved in.'

She raised an eyebrow, shuffled through the manila folder in front of her, eyeing the papers intently. 'I'm pretty interested in that myself. I'm going to have to go through everything you've got.'

'Happy to share.'

'And get off the case.'

George drank more of his coffee. Then he drank the water to get rid of the taste.

'I like to finish the job I've been hired to do,' he said. 'Get to the truth of it. Especially when it's for an old friend.'

'I get it,' Lewis replied, 'no one likes to be pulled off a case, but there's been a murder now, it's no longer the case you were hired for. We will take it from here.'

'I won't get in your way. I could help you. As you've seen I'm more than happy to cooperate.'

'I've told you to steer clear, and I only give sensible advice, but ultimately it's up to you whether you continue to investigate this or not. This is complicated now.'

'I have a client, if she wants me to continue, I'll continue. If not, I won't.'

She nodded. 'I can only offer my advice. And I've given it. You'd be better off making friends with the force here.'

'I'm not here to make friends. I'm here for the truth.'

Lewis looked at him for a short, intense moment, eyes like a spotlight, before opening the folder again.

They went over the details and then she left him alone under the searching bright lights.

Bodies, living and dead, are natural storytellers. It takes just one-tenth of a second to form a first impression of someone. Movement is vocabulary, all cells gregarious. It was only understanding the messages that took time: translation was the tricky business, George knew.

Bodies tell stories without wanting to. There is little we can do to stop them. Yet detecting a liar by body language alone is almost worse than chance, George knew from his textbooks. We can't — unless maybe we're a highly trained CIA operative working in the field every day — predict whether someone is lying or telling the truth, any better than if we, say, flipped a coin. It's not a question of observation. One can be observant enough to spot the cues associated with stress — slower natural movements, pauses in speech — ultimately it comes down to psychology. That's the reason lie detector tests are inadmissible in court. Human psychology contains multitudes, and ciphering each individual's codes is near impossible. A loved one, who we know bodily and intimately, can lie to our faces without us realising.

Chance. Yes. Yet there were certain bodily cues that George had learned were associated with lying if he knew the normal baseline, as opposed to a simple concealment of the truth: shorter answers, reduction of movement in the arms, legs, feet and hands, faster speech rate, a higher voice pitch. The brain uses its cognitive energy on the complex task of invention, which is harder to do than simply denying the truth — so it slows down all the other processes. But, as George had learned through field work, this wasn't universally the case, and intellectually isolating these elements led, if anything, to a reduction in overall understanding of the scene. By focusing so narrowly, you became numb to anything else, the broader and sometimes more meaningful cues, that might be going on around you.

So he'd chucked it. The laser focus. Trying to tunnel and classify cues that might not even be there at all. He'd come to rely on his gut, and let his intellect give way to instinct, taking in the whole scene, opening up his mind to see something of the truth. He did deep breathing. Visualised. Relaxed into a state of open meditation.

He was preparing to do this now. He'd left the mainland and Lewis and was back on Songbird Island, sitting near a bush peppered with flowers, their tiny yellow petals aching for the sun, grassy stems feral under the sea winds.

He needed distance, mental, and physical. Surfing had always been that for him. An active meditation. Nature was good. Nature with a physical activity was best of all. He couldn't surf now, but he could hike.

So he buttoned up his light blue shirt, strapped on his sandals, grabbed his backpack and left. Paloma had told him about a mountain trail, steep and long, not far from the main house.

The regular tread of his feet was a kind of hypnosis as he stalked out from the house to find the track.

Everything gradually stilled as he walked, and he came to a large map with the various hiking trails laid out in coloured codes. He took the right fork, the blue trail, that would take him up to the mountaintop, and felt his mind quieten and senses open up as nature encircled him. He passed a globular middle-aged man in beige shorts, face full of effort and sun; then two joggers in lycra, sneakers, with hard legs and hard faces, then no one.

Thick bush spanned either side of the dirt track. The rainforest floor was covered in layers of leaves, soft and dormant. A million living things lived under there, if he'd care to look — some friendly, some not. George was interested in the sensation of his legs as they walked, the sound of his breathing, of the things he felt, now he was quiet.

He thought about what Songbird Island would have been like before Europeans came. Before anything was built here, before the resort, before colonisation. The path spoke of humans but the windward lean of the trees, the ocean in the distance, the tawny birds in underbrush, legs thin as the delicate branches; the leaves, clustered, amicable; the rich soil of the fervid earth; these were specimens of that last world, the thousand quietnesses that stilled the loud thoughts and feelings of the present. He understood why so many poets were devoted solo pedestrians. It was impossible to walk, like this, with another person. Thoughts were always leaning to that person, or the way you appeared to the person, a self-consciousness of some kind was necessary. On a good walk, there is no self-consciousness. No self.

The wind wound above him in sighs, and the path got steeper. The sea started to become more visible too, between the waving eucalypts, a slice of turquoise through the leaves.

It became rockier, peaks and castles breaking through the earth and between trees, iron grey, sharp as teeth. There was a rustle of movement somewhere in the bush, or was it further up the path? Some animal.

The trees thinned and the mountain face thickened as he moved further up towards the summit. Dark caves were pocked into the rock, the path got wispier. Large round boulders stacked on iron-coloured shelves. As he moved upwards the birds scattered ahead at pace; the branches arching with each departure.

To his right, curving bushland so thick it seemed almost solid. To the left, the ocean, glassy and smooth. Ahead, the jagged steps of rock petered out, padded with dusty soil. He saw a ringed lookout, with a warning sign in cautious red.

He was at the summit, and his breath came sharp and hot. He looked down, and could make out the Knightley house as a lonely square of white, a distant ringed circus. The ocean was vast. So much more of it than land, the distant islands, mostly small and uninhabited, were nothing more than dropped pebbles of green in the sea, sinking more each day. Water was the dominant force. It seemed wrong to call the planet 'Earth', when it was so clearly ruled by water.

He took a long guzzle of his water, tasting warm plastic. He closed his eyes, and sat for a moment.

He focused on his breath. He imagined breathing in white light, felt it curl in his stomach and slowly extend to his feet. He calmed his mind, watching thoughts come and go, letting them fall away.

Soon they stilled and the world outside of his own mind — the sweep of the waves, the warm sound of bees in yellow flowers, the yelps of people in the ocean, the distant hum of golf buggy and birdsong — all, all fell out of his scope of focus. Instead, he was aware of the inner motion of breath, and then not even that.

After a time, he willed a thought up out of nothing and prayed, or asked, or perhaps it was both: *Help me to see what really is.*

He opened his eyes, and it was almost a surprise to see the world there after all: the same sea, the same bee-buzzing flowers. He'd been somewhere else, but where? He padded back down the path and went back to the house.

As he walked into the room to talk to Walt, George passively let the impressions in. Ease, affluence. The entitlement of a vast building ringed by lush tropical flowers, white and steady while trampled underfoot.

That perfectly ordered, shining strawberry hair. A

bunch of pink roses frothing from a vase on the table. The pin-sharp shirt, the crisp, glinting watch and clipped fingernails.

George felt himself attracted and repelled by the man. His good looks were seductive, confident. And yet there was something else too, as there sometimes is in confident men. His eyes were cold and domineering, and there was a discord between them and his lips, which formed a welcoming smile. They could have belonged to two different people.

'You wanted to talk? What can I do for you?'

Walt was sitting at Tom's desk with easy belonging. George wondered if he'd ever felt out of place a day in his entire life. Was he jealous? Or suspicious? Or both?

'Well, we have to clear up this mess,' George said. 'I have a confession to make.'

'Should the police be here?' asked Walt.

'No, nothing like that. I'm a private investigator.'

Walt looked at other man smoothly. He didn't seem surprised.

'I see. Why the ruse?'

'I told Paloma it would be best to keep it quiet. She asked me to come up here for a small matter, but, well, the matter seems anything but small now.'

'Bad business,' agreed Walt. He was composed, not giving anything away. That was his baseline.

'I thought it might help if I continue to look into the situation, alongside the police. Paloma agrees.'

'Any help is good,' Walt said, expectant.

'So it might help if we have a talk.'

'Shoot.'

'You look after the day-to-day here on the island, is that right?'

'Yes, I make sure it's all running as it should be, that our guests are getting what they need and want. If I have good people, my job's easy.'

'Must be boring after a while, I'd imagine.'

'No two days are the same. I like it, I can split my time between here and Sydney, and Celine prefers the island to the city at the moment, so it works for both of us.'

'You've been in the same role a long time then? No desire to move up the ladder to CEO, slip into Tom's shoes?'

'I don't flatter myself that I could,' he said politely. 'There are others way more *qualified*. I like my job. I've never needed to move up the ladder as you put it.'

'How in touch are you with what's going on at HQ?'

'These days it doesn't matter where in the world you are really. Offices will soon be a thing of the past.'

'You get back there how often?'

'Every fortnight or so. Meetings still have to be had. Though the business is much less bureaucratic than most, Old Mate was progressive like that.'

'So you're involved with all the finances?'

'We each have our own areas we look after, with a fair bit of autonomy. Old Mate knew that the best managers delegate. Sydney managers do their own thing, and I get on with mine. Together we're a seamless machine.'

'How easily then could someone exploit the system?'

'Given the right knowledge, I guess they possibly could. I haven't thought about it. We're a close-knit team. Family and long termers for the most part.'

'How well did you know Adam?'

'He was my assistant for, oh, about a year now.'

'You trusted him?'

'I did, to my discredit. Yes, I trusted him. I wouldn't have employed him otherwise.'

'The reason I came up here is that Paloma received a letter, and to put it bluntly, it accused you of embezzling money from the business.' Here George felt something nameless shift in Walt's demeanour. Shock?

'It did?' Walt said, the smile on his lips not fading, instead taking on a sharper aspect.

'Who do you think would make these kinds of accusations? Any past employees with a grudge?'

Walt stroked his face. 'Not that I can think of. No bad breaks or anything like that. No one with any cause to be bitter. I mean, apart from Adam, who was clearly unhinged and had something against me.'

'My thoughts exactly,' said George. 'Does the name Phoebe Harris mean anything to you?'

'Harris . . .' Walt repeated, slowly, his hand still on his broad chin. 'Should it?'

'How about Gregg Coleman?'

George's senses felt a tweak, a small moment that felt . . . different. Walt's face looked the same, looking at George quietly, thinking.

'Not sure. Who is it?'

'Sean Longworth?' The nameless something grew.

'No. Nothing.'

'Might be nothing, you sure don't remember those names?'

'I deal with hundreds, thousands of names every year. As I said, they don't ring any particular bells.'

'As part of the investigations, my Sydney colleagues are looking into all personal expenses, travel, vendor approvals, that sort of thing. Most can be done centrally and electronically, however someone will be in touch about accessing any hard copies they might need from here. That okay with you?'

'Of course,' he said, calmly. 'Is that it?'

'I told you it'd be easy. The Sydney folks may have a few things to cross-check with you, after.'

'Fine,' he said, and rose, his face cool and fair.

—

George stopped by to check in on Celine.

She was in bed, napping he first thought, but she stirred when he came in.

Her skin looked like parchment, dry and subtly textured in the sunny light of her room, no makeup, and she was maybe the most beautiful woman in the whole world.

'Hello, hero,' she said softly. A book lay open beside her. 'I don't want to disturb you, I'm sorry.'

'Come in,' she said, patting a spot on her cool linen sheets.

He sat.

'You okay?'

'The doctor said I'll be fine. The drug's basically working its way out of my system now.'

'And otherwise?'

'I'm a selfish woman, aren't I?' she said. 'I want everything. Why is that? Who am I to deserve it? Don't I already have enough?'

'We all make mistakes. Lord knows I have. Only a problem if we don't learn from them.'

She smiled at that. 'I'm better at making other things. People, for one, I mean look at Jude. He's perfect.'

'Perfect's a hard word to live up to for a kid.'

'What did your mum think of you?'

'Ha, well, it wasn't that I was perfect, that's for sure. And with plenty of good reasons, I'm afraid.'

'And what did you think of your mum when you were a kid?'

'That she was a bogan Botticelli,' he answered with a smile.

Celine laughed.

'I'm done with all that,' she said, suddenly serious. 'Men. Just me and Walt and Jude.'

'Okay, Celine.'

She lowered her voice. 'Find out, will you?'

It was noon — the kind of tropical noon when the sun turns savage, stabbing through clouds.

George wanted to get away, away from the investigation, away from circular, suspicious thoughts;

mostly, he wanted to get away from feeling as though he couldn't do anything about anything. The police had advised him to stop investigating. He wouldn't.

He also knew he wouldn't have those thoughts, not those exact ones, and possibly not even variations, if he moved, put himself somewhere else.

He'd seen so many victims in his time, not only of crimes, also of mental states, heads full of negativity, unconsciously and endlessly repeating damage by seeing themselves as victims. Depression and anxiety became familiar, rage and sadness the predictable result.

It was a challenge in his line of work. Saw the worst of people, but in a way, now he almost needed it, a kind of test of his resolve. George was scared that he hadn't beaten the urge to fall into gloom; to blame others for his situation in life, to crave darkness — and so he tested himself. Over and over.

Memories tested him most of all. Back in his room, he let one in.

They were younger, Paloma had lighter hair, George more of it. Hers was tucked into her camel winter coat, they were in Paris.

Everything about her looked expensive, at home. Among the well-designed things, the reticent yet froufrou beauty of Paris, with its endless iron Juliet balconies and its hidden courtyards, she seemed at home. George was angry and tired — what about? He couldn't recall now. Jet-lagged, maybe, or just pissed at the impenetrability of things. He hated the stupid hidden courtyards and the elegant balconies and the bags worth more than his car, and the eyes always on you. He was tired and wanted everything porous, self-explanatory, and he refused to go to the Louvre with her. He boiled the kettle in the hotel room and drank a cup of plain hot water as he watched her walk out of their room, then caught a glimpse of her — as strangers would — on the street below. With her string bag and determined walk. He could pick her walk anywhere — didn't even need to see her. Could hear that familiar pace and slight shuffle where she dragged her heels. No one had told him that was what love was like: knowing and adoring the sound of someone else's walk. He was suddenly feeling bereft. He knew she'd be happy enough, walking alone, going to the Louvre alone. Suddenly he wasn't happy to be sitting there with his hot water and his view — now sans Paloma — with the smell of expensive hotel AC.

He put on his shoes and ran after her, as if his life depended on it, through the unfamiliar streets that all looked the same. His phone wouldn't pick up Google Maps so he guessed at which way she'd walk. Boys stared as he ran, maybe wondering if he'd committed a crime. She couldn't be too far ahead, he thought. And then he saw her familiar coat and the way her hair tucked into the back of it, the glint of her shiny boots, the swing of her string bag, and he felt relief.

'Hey,' he called. She was startled for a brief moment, then smiled widely, 'Oh, hi. So the lure of the Louvre was too much after all?'

'Louvre? Oh yeah, that too I suppose,' he said, and she clutched his arm and George felt everything was alright with the world. It wasn't, but sometimes there's beauty in lies.

What had made that memory come to George now, on the island, in her world? That he had chased after her? That he had realised his stupid mistake only after he'd made it? That he'd done something, that time? That he hadn't done anything at all the next time? That he'd let her go? More than that. He'd made her leave. Put it onto her.

They'd spent a few weeks in France, yet there were only one or two other vivid memories of that time.

He'd spent their time at the Louvre looking at her, mostly, and marvelling at the sheer wildness that two people could ever fall in love, continue to be in love. When they had come out of the gallery there was blinding rain. He wasn't dressed for it, and bought a cheap transparent umbrella from one of the tourist stands nearby, and they laughed, getting wet, as they walked through the Tuileries, then stopped at a café for mulled wine. The waiter openly admired Paloma, effusively polite and solicitous as he delivered their glasses, asked where they (she) was from, and were all Australian women like her?

'I'm right here, dude,' George said as he sidled off.

'He's charming!'

'Oh very.' George smiled, and gulped his hot wine.

They'd gone back to the hotel for a long afternoon of skin, rain on windows, peony petals, expensive sheets, mouths warm with wine and spice.

He wondered again: *Why am I recalling this now? It's not as if it's any sort of revelation.* He didn't always know himself, but he know *this* about himself: that he had lost Paloma because he wasn't honest with himself or with her, and he had given her no choice. That was the profound regret he lived with every day.

—

Paloma appeared at his doorway, as if conjured by his memories.

'I suppose you've got your own reasons for not telling me about Cee,' she said. 'And Adam.' She looked at him coolly.

'Client confidentiality,' he replied.

'So she's a client?'

'Not technically. Habit, I suppose.'

'You don't need to tell me everything. Anything except what I pay you to. It's Cee. My sister, George. I could've helped her. I can help her.'

'Maybe she didn't want you to know. Maybe she was ashamed.'

'Ashamed? You don't know Cee,' she sat on the bed.

'Well maybe she felt like you didn't need another problem in your life right now. Maybe she was protecting you.'

'That's fair enough. But it doesn't hurt any less.'

'You didn't tell her about the letters.'

'That's different,' she said, looking stung.

'You should talk to her. You okay?' George sat on the bed. Paloma stood up.

'Why can't things be simple?'

'When are things ever simple?'

'Some things are simple,' she said. 'It's everything we build up that gets complicated.' She paused. 'How did *we* get so complicated, George?' — then quickly continued, 'Don't answer that.'

'But I want to.' He replied, reaching for her hand. 'I had so much bullshit going on in my own head, back then. Stuff that had absolutely nothing to do with you. I got in my own way, I thought I was trapped, that things would never change, that you were stopping me from being my true self. I couldn't see that you were the only one who knew my true self. I'm the one who messed it up, and I'll never be more sorry about anything.'

'It was a long time ago.'

'I'm sorry.'

'I know you are.'

She pulled her hand away and disappeared like smoke.

10.

Life in board shorts and bikinis lulled you into a sense of protection, insulated you against extremes. It was all too easy, when the days were a humid mid-twenties, season in season out, to start to relax into the consistency, to think nothing could ever disturb the calm. Bursts of sub-tropical rain during the wet season were soon forgotten, sand drying out under the dazzling sun.

But the locals knew better. Despite being sheltered from the worst storms, Songbird Islanders had seen their share, huddling in bathtubs as the sound of the wind assailed every sense, striking their hearts with primal fear. They'd never been too badly hit, but Paloma knew the sounds and fears of cyclones deep in her being.

The winds were changing. She had that familiar feeling, of trapped heat and still air, a storm ache, the sense of a sword about to drop. She was used to that by now, with her anxiety. It comforted her somehow, that the external atmosphere finally matched her inner condition.

Paloma scrolled through the *Daily Mercury*, clicked 'Cyclone Lucie: Latest BOM Warnings'. Phrases like 'hours of terror' and 'Premier urges residents to stay put' and 'Category 3 and intensifying' and 'heading south' sunk in. The sky was operatic outside her window.

At the house, the energy was contained, thrumming. What had already been a tense atmosphere was now bubbling, threatening to blow up. The family had gathered around a laptop in the kitchen, the unceasing winds outside, watching the latest news.

'We're in the warning zone now,' Celine said. The criss-cross of lines under her eyes were more prominent. Paloma put her arm around her sister.

'How bad is it?' Iris asked. She too looked pinched.

'Not good, but not too bad yet,' Celine said. 'We may need to evacuate the guests soon, but for now it looks like it's not swinging directly our way.'

The TV news anchor's voice rang out.

'Lucie is forecast to make landfall on the mainland as a severe tropical cyclone in the next thirty-six hours. Gales are expected to extend to the exposed coast and islands elsewhere tomorrow morning and early afternoon. The Bureau of Meteorology believes the cyclone will make landfall during abnormally high-tides, worsening the scenario.'

They crossed to Walt as a spokesperson for Songbird Island.

'The island has activated all steps in line with cyclone policies and procedures,' Walt said. 'We are well prepared for these events and have processes in place to deal with current conditions. Safety for all guests and staff is our highest priority.

'All guests have been advised to remain in their rooms or the main hall area of the main hotel for the time being, all are cyclone resilient. How long this continues is dependent on the path of the cyclone in the next twenty-four hours.'

—

George was on his laptop in his room.

'You see the news?' Paloma asked.

'Yeah. Looks like Lucie's main brunt will miss the island, so that's good news.'

'It's unpredictable,' she said. 'We just have to wait it out. We'll know for sure by tomorrow, it could still easily head this way. Whatever happens it's not going to be good.'

'You worried?' he asked, closing his laptop softly, like hands in prayer.

'I suppose.'

'What do we do, in the meantime?' he asked. Paloma let the question float away.

'How's the investigation going?' She asked, sitting on the bed.

'Nothing new. I'm waiting for the forensics to get back with some info.'

'Paloma,' he said, looking at her closely. 'Tell me to fuck off, but are you okay?'

'What do you mean?'

'I'm worried. Your panic attack the other day, the diving, and it could be nothing but I've noticed when you eat you . . . don't eat.'

So he had noticed. Paloma supposed it should have been no surprise, after all he was a detective.

'It hasn't been easy, this last year,' she said, unsure of where to start, where to end. 'But I'd rather be sick and happy than sick and unhappy.'

'Are you sick?'

'I never used to be, I was a picture of health.'

'And that's changed?'

'I got weird.'

'You were always weird,' he said with a gentle smile. 'Are you happy?'

'Oh, no.' she said. 'Grief works in mysterious ways. In ways I couldn't predict, things have happened to me. I never would have thought I'd be . . .' she trailed off.

'Anxiety is a normal reaction to grief. Most of us at one point or another experience it.'

But she didn't want to hear his platitudes.

'George,' she lay back on the bed, looking at the ceiling. 'It's not just that. Sometimes I think that my brain chemistry has changed. I wonder if I'll ever be the same person again. I think the other me is gone.'

'Maybe she is. So what?' He lay back too.

'I liked her. She was happy.'

'She was deluded.'

'What?' Paloma looked at him, surprised.

'No offence, my love. You may have travelled the world, but you didn't know the world. Not really. You were born with everything. Rich, white, good looking, a loving family. You never had to work for a thing, never had to see that the world wasn't a beautiful place. Or, not only a beautiful place. I don't envy you that. I never did. Because when you inevitably found out that things aren't always wonderful, when disaster struck, you weren't equipped to deal with it. How could you be?'

'I don't know,' she said, tired. 'Maybe you're right. I don't want to have this dread all the time, George. I don't want to be thinking that everything can, and will, kill me. Yet how can I not? We can die so easily. Literally *anything* at *any time* could do it. I don't know how to live that way. It's too much to live with all the time. It's too heavy to take on.'

Paloma looked at him, thinking.

'Yes, we're all going to die,' he said calmly. 'But we should live anyway.'

She kissed him. Not only because of her desire for him but as proof of life, of living anyway. Was it stupid? Probably. What's new. He kissed her back some.

All she knew was that when she thought of him, it was of sprawling, vivid, earthy things: light, warmth, elements, the conditions for growth.

He put his hands on her and it was all so familiar, new too — a live-wire of desire singing itself through her veins and nerve endings. Her skin shivered and the thunder growled low outside, and she smelled the ozone of the coming rain and the patchouli scent of his skin.

—

Paloma and George, naked under the sheets. Paloma thought: *Perhaps now it'll be all languorous sensuality, extempore sweet-nothings, hiding out together as the storm passes.*

'There's a point around here I want to surf,' he said.

'Okay,' she replied, drowsily, full of sun.

'With the change in winds, it should be getting some really good waves, I mean spectacular waves, it's really a once-in-a-lifetime opportunity,' he said with intensity.

'Wait,' she said, as if waking, 'You mean *right now?* In the cyclone?'

'It's not as dangerous as it sounds. I know what I'm doing, and if I go this afternoon before the cyclone fully hits . . .'

'Are you kidding me?' She asked, burning hot, feeling that nothing had changed, in all these years, he still wanted just that, that one thing. Surf. To the detriment of everything else. Every*one* else.

'You've got to be fucking kidding me.'

'I realise how it sounds, Pal, but I wouldn't do anything risky. Well, not too risky. I know my limits, I know the sea —'

'It doesn't matter what I say, does it?'

'Of course it does.'

'Okay then. Don't go.'

'Paloma —'

'It's so incredibly stupid. Surfing in a cyclone! Why would you even consider it?'

'I can handle myself. I've surfed big, bigger in fact —'

'I know you can, I know you have, this is different, it's unpredictable. You could actually *die*.'

'You're being dramatic,' he said gently.

That was what pushed her over the edge.

'Don't condescend to me,' she said, getting out of bed, hastily pulling on her clothes. 'You absolute bastard. Do whatever you like.'

———

Paloma walked blindly up to her room, repeating *the idiot. The stupid idiot.*

She pulled her covers up over her head and in her cocoon her phone flashed. It was a text from the island's security:

DISASTER PLAN UPGRADED.
EVACUATION PROCEDURES NOW IN
EFFECT.

Paloma groaned. Sighed. Emerged, splashed her face, looked at her dark circles, put on some concealer, and headed downstairs in search of Cee.

'Of course we're not bloody going,' said Cee. 'The guests have started evacuating now, but we'll stay put. We'll get everyone else out, then we'll batten down the hatches. We're staying home.'

No one argued. The wind was sounding more and more furious, like an engine revving, the windows beginning to shake, the sky dark as twilight.

'This island's cursed,' Iris said dramatically, her excitement gone.

They put on parkas and boots, Celine overseeing

the guests evacuating to the mainland in groups. Emergency supplies, including meal packs and cyclone kits, had been hauled out for those staying the night.

Iris, Walt, the remaining staff and Paloma headed out on the beachfront, sandbagging, removing outdoor furniture and anything that might topple or go flying, parking golf buggies in the lee of the bungalows. Wind and rain whipped Paloma's face and stung her eyes, the beach a blur and hum of noise. She tried not to think of George. George's hair, George's lips, George's fucking cheekbones.

It was getting worse, fast.

She was getting scared to be outside, but there were the few end bungalows to secure. At the last one on the strip, she moved the potted plants and outdoor furniture inside as quickly as she could and wrestled with a hammock against the whipping wind. Reaching up to unlock it from the front beam, her eyes blurred with rain, she thought saw the sudden rush of something coming towards her, then felt a searing, piercing pain on the side of her head. Falling onto the porch, she felt a moment of terror and then everything was quiet and soft and dark.

11.

Everything outside the window was iron grey, sea waves tipped with dirty oyster peaks, sky and earth indistinguishable in the misty haze of wind-churned wet air, battering the glass. George felt shut-up and sour. It was sordid somehow, being inside, the pool of coffee in his cup, his rumpled T-shirt like an antimacassar on the cane chair.

He was irritated, too, that the gold of that moment — with Paloma — had faded so fast. He could feel the sea heaving outside like it was a disembodied part of himself, a vein run riot with nature, and he felt shimmering and restless. He checked the conditions, again, on his phone. *I'd better move fast now.*

Maybe he'd always be alone. Maybe it would be always just him and the sea. There was nothing for him to do now, except do it. He put on a wetsuit and bolted down the stairs. It'd taken a bit of manoeuvring to get a board. Eventually he'd found a bemused local who had one — the rental fee unquestionably steep at $350. He figured he'd never see either of them again, George supposed.

As George left, his golf-buggy radio spewed *All*

You Need Is Love, clogging up his thoughts. What kind of sick universe would play that song right here, right now?

Outside everything had a wild, on-the-edge energy, the amiable tropics transformed into something darker. He felt his pulse thrum, his eyes sting in the horizontal rain and seawater.

The break was on the other side of the island, was a twenty-or-so minute drive from the main house on a buggy, on a good day. George had a struggle strapping on the board so it didn't fly off. Once it was secured he took off on the wet road, feeling like the buggy would tip on the sharper turns and with every gust.

I love Paloma, he thought. *Still. Or again. Yeah, and so what?* It didn't make a bit of difference. He'd get over it. He didn't feel calm or optimistic. The wild birds dug up their voices in alarm, sputtered into the wind.

When he arrived at the spot, all of it seemed so distant. Paloma, Adam's body, Celine, Walt, even his own empty Sydney life — all he felt now was the rain on his skin, like bullets, all he could see was the waves. *Oh God, the waves!*

Standing in the storm, looking out on the dark, perfect waves glistening and misty, promising a good ride, a great ride. The sky was dark against the turquoise sea, thrashing. It had never looked more beautiful.

He ran down to the beach fighting for every step, then plunged, paddled as quickly as he could. He paddled forever, face battered again and again with water.

Finally in position, he saw a wave. Nice take off, he pulled straight in deep into the tube, the barrel trying to clamp down on him, but he drove through and out on the open face. He held the line, re-adjusting nicely.

His skin thrummed. He caught another wave, the sky lightening now with ribbons of sun, prismatic in the churning sea. Wind loud and grating, his ears were complaining and cold. The lights on the island became a scribble, blurred in the shadowy foreshore.

Still he surfed, exhilarated, violently cutting through the waves.

Feel the wind, breathe in. Focus on the breath.

His muscle memory took over, his mind hit a plane of pure light, even as the world was dark in the gloom. Here, now, his body and nature coexisted, indistinguishable, everything porous and pliable, like those fleeting moments he sometimes had of intense empathy for everything, everyone everywhere, knowing that they were him and wanting to help them all. Those moments were all too rare, but here he was, part of the ocean. He felt that moment. And it was beautiful.

Then, it was as if the blood drained from his body into the sea. *What am I doing?* Here he was when Paloma, the woman he loved (again, still) needed him? When they'd shared a genuine moment of connection after being apart for so long, when she'd let him in to something intimate, telling him about her dad, her grief, her changes. He had left. He, who supposedly looked for enlightenment and redemption, but who just lived out the same patterns again, again, again.

He felt chilled and clumsily peeled off his wetsuit

with numb hands. He attempted to put the surfboard back on the buggy, but the wind whipped it out of his hands, sharply digging into his ribs, and he abandoned it on the sand.

He struggled to drive the buggy against the wind, fearing it would be blown off the road into the cliffs below at any moment. He left it, walked the rest of the way, nearly blinded by rain, cursing his stupidity. By the time he got back to the house the energy had changed.

Towelling himself off in his room, he checked his phone and saw a text from DI Lewis:

We need to talk. Tried calling, reception unreliable. We can't get across to the island till it passes. Have made discovery on case, relevant info on Walt, be wary until we arrive. Stay safe.

He went to look for Paloma.

12.

But she wasn't there.

13.

'Where's Paloma?'

Celine was coming back up to the main house carrying garden chairs.

'Up at the bungalows, making sure everything is secure,' Celine replied. 'Why?'

But George had already taken off.

Nearing the neat row of identical bungalows, he strained for signs of her through the lashing rain. The first was empty, the second too. At the third he saw a hammock being thrashed by the wind, half unhooked from its post, and a shape on the deck: Paloma.

She was unconscious, blood and water on her face.

'Paloma,' he shouted, his hands going numb. 'Can you hear me?'

She didn't respond. He checked her airway — clear. Pulse — slow, he thought, but okay. She was alive. He needed to get a medic but he couldn't leave her alone out here like this. He checked the bungalow door, locked. *Fuck.* He decided to take her back up to the house.

George carefully rolled Paloma on to her side, watching her closely for any changes. When there were none, he gently, slowly, pulled her up and into his arms, her face close to his, her skin plastered with black hair.

'Oh my God, what happened?' Celine ran to George when she saw him coming up the path, dropping the garden tools she had been carrying.

'I don't know, I found her up at one of the bungalows. She's unconscious. Get a paramedic over here, now!'

George went inside and placed Paloma gently on a big sofa in the front living room, blotching the fabric with water. He could hear Celine on the phone, voice raised in panic.

'They're coming,' Celine said, leaning down to stroke Paloma's face, her hands shaking. Then she left again.

George covered Paloma with a throw, and Celine reappeared with towels and a bowl of water, which she used to gently clean Paloma's head. The bleeding had stopped, and Celine cleaned the wound as gently as she could.

The island's paramedic was probably quick to arrive, though it didn't feel that way to George, who watched every rise and fall of Paloma's chest intently, straining to see any signs of consciousness.

The paramedic calmly checked her over, a kit by his knee.

'She's stable,' he said, 'And there's no signs of spinal injury. Looks like she's had a nasty blow to the head. We'll need to get her to a hospital ASAP.'

'No one's going anywhere tonight,' Celine said.

'Can you stay here and keep an eye on her until we can get out?'

The paramedic agreed and consented to moving Paloma up to her bedroom away from the more vulnerable front of the house.

In her bedroom, head bandaged, Paloma was the one point of stillness in a world charged with panic, movement, the noise of wind.

Someone had turned on a battery-powered radio, the emergency warning signal slicing through the house. George left Paloma with the medic to see how else he could help. The cyclone was close.

He found Celine in the front of the house, taping up a window with an X.

'What can I do?' he asked, desperate.

'Fill the buckets in the kitchen with water. And all the baths,' she said.

He was grateful to have a role, and busied himself with the assignment, finding Jude unplugging appliances in the kitchen.

'This is pretty intense, huh?' Jude said, looking worried beneath the lopsided smile.

'This building was made to last,' said George. 'Nothing to worry about.'

'How's Aunty Paloma? Mum told me she hit her head.'

George stared into the bucket he was filling. 'She'll be alright. How many baths do you have? And where are they?'

'You want to take a bath?' Jude asked, incredulous.

'To fill up with water, in case it gets cut off.'

'Oh, right. Don't worry about it. I'll do it. There's like, a million. Or at least five,' and he left on his task.

George heard someone fighting the front door as they came in, struggling to close it again.

'Whew!' Walt called. 'Power's off now ladies and gents. Hope you all charged your phones.'

George checked his phone. It blinked with a text from the lead in the forensic accountants team:

We need to talk asap. I rang earlier and got your voicemail.

George tried to call back, was immediately cut off. Reception was now non-existent.

'George,' Celine came into the kitchen. 'We're all going to hole up in the main foyer. Come when you're ready.'

The day was getting even darker. As George finished filling the buckets, it had turned into an eerie pinkish twilight. In the main foyer he found Walt, Celine, Jude, and Iris, looking anxious yet almost festive, with their makeshift camp out. Iris was drinking a huge glass of wine, wrapped in a blanket. The foyer, out of the range of any windows, was enormous, and furnished with two sofas, the floor scattered with huge cushions. There were water bottles, wine bottles, a battery-operated radio blaring, torches, hurricane lanterns, food, candles and blankets.

'I've got to be with Paloma,' he said. 'I'll take a few bits up there.'

'Come down if anything changes with her okay?' Celine said.

George nodded, grabbed a bottle of water, snacks, a few candles and a hurricane lantern.

'See you soon,' he said, and went upstairs.

Paloma was still unconscious, the medic anxious-eyed through his professional calm. A book on his lap, a lantern on the table beside him.

'Here we go,' George said, grim. He pulled a wicker chair beside Paloma and held her hand.

The winds were wild and then wilder, the sound roaring to a volume George wouldn't have believed possible, the roar of a 747. He could hear the house groan and windows shake, the sound of bangs and yells, the sweep of rain and trees outside, possibly roof panels and buggies too.

Don't let it end like this, he prayed to the wind, to the rain, to the sky, to all things watery and inconstant. The house could take a hell of a beating, so could he. The wind and fury outside had conjured a primal fear in George, who knew that fear of nature was not only the correct attitude, but also a kind of respect. He'd seen enough to know that if nature wanted you gone, you were gone. If it decided that it'd had enough of humanity, it wouldn't have a problem wiping us all out.

But it couldn't end like this, with Paloma hurt. With Paloma hurt by him, again.

He held on to her hand and whispered a mantra or a prayer as the cyclone passed overhead. *I'm sorry. I'm sorry. I'm sorry.*

The afternoon turned to a night that seemed

endless, lit by weak pools of light from the hurricane lanterns. The wind died off, and then picked up again all night. George curled up beside Paloma on the bed on top of the covers. He couldn't sleep more than a few moments at a time, and even then his dreams were full of broken doors, smashed windows and an unrelenting wind taking everything away.

—

As soon as transport was given the okay the following day, Paloma was moved to the mainland hospital. She was still unconscious.

'She's had a traumatic brain injury,' the doctor told Celine and George, 'a hard blow to the head with blunt trauma. Her eyes open to stimulation, which is a good sign, but we still need to closely monitor her, as the brain can have an inflammatory response to injuries like these up to five days later, and that can be more dangerous than the initial trauma. It's a waiting game. She's in the best possible place, and she's on sedation and pain medication. She's comfortable.'

George sat by Paloma's hospital bedside: unslept, unshaven, unhinged.

Hooked up to tubes and machines, her wrist plastered in tape, spots of dried blood underneath, Paloma's sweeping dark eyelashes were closed on her too-white cheeks.

—

He'd lost control over things with Paloma at the end, back in Sydney, and that's what he replayed in his mind while he watched lying in her hospital bed. Kicking himself while down.

When they had lived together, things as incremental and imperceptible as the Earth's rotation — and just as inevitable — had started to grind into George. He'd begun to feel that he needed to apologise for things that he decided to do — staying out, going away, leaving her behind, obsessing about the surf, not spending time with her. She always knew she shared George with the ocean, the other love of his life, and George had always considered it a pretty equal split, but he sometimes wondered if he was addicted to surfing. She was never demanding; she never said she needed more from him. He had subconscious ideas of what a relationship should be, of what he, as a partner, should be. And he felt he was falling short. That was the start of the end.

No, George thought, watching her breath. *Think of something else. Think of before that.* He sat under the harsh lights amid the comings and goings of medical staff, the constant beat of the machines and ever-moving lines of the monitors.

A mate had lent them his shack down south for the summer. It was almost a treehouse, perched among eucalypts with a wide wooden porch, all hand-hewn wood and warm corners nestled among gum and fruit trees, the sun lurking in wide panes, deep slow-shifting shadows glowing across the strawberry patch by the front window, across the oranges in the fruit bowl on the table that Paloma had picked. It was off a dirt road just back from the beach that didn't get any traffic, the waves were insanely fun every day and all you could hear were birds — the rooster in the mornings, chatty rainbow lorikeets streaking the skies, the comforting warble of magpies — and the whispering sea as you went to sleep at night.

Paloma was still jet-lagged after travelling for a shoot, and when they arrived in the afternoon she had a shower and went directly, naked, into bed while he watched a lilac thunderstorm roll in. He knew then that this was it: the bubble he wanted to be in forever.

He was nervous, and distracted himself cutting up all the fruit they had, piles and piles of strawberries, oranges, apples into huge mounds, packing them into bowls and Tupperware while he waited for her to wake up.

She'd never let him live that down, his nervous fruit salad energy, as he waited that afternoon to ask her to marry him. They ate the fruit for days until it grew soft, bruised and brown and they had to throw it away. It was the happiest time of his life.

After that golden summer, they came back to Sydney and normal life resumed. Surfing took off on a new level; George got a high-profile sponsor, he was earning more money, and getting more publicity and attention, all things he'd never really experienced and had no idea what to do with.

When Paloma wanted to set a date for the wedding he put it off, thinking of all the things he had to do first, the comps, the travel, things that never ended, and so he delayed it.

He had never seen himself as the type of man who would be married. As time lengthened and distractions mounted, he realised that while he loved her, he was falling out of love with the idea of being a married man. He didn't want to stay home. He wanted to make the most of this, probably short-lived, window of success. That the idea and the reality of marriage weren't one and the same never occurred to him. So he backed off. He spent all his time surfing, doing publicity, hanging out with the surf crew, heading off on trips. He barely recognised what he was doing at the time. He was dazzled by newfound wealth and minor celebrity, the flattering hangers on, the esteem of being someone who people wanted to be with, who they looked up to.

He couldn't help it. He remembered a conversation with hot shame.

Is it another woman?

At the time he had reacted angrily, the accused, stormed off and felt vindicated. Later he thought: *It's not a woman. It's women, the idea that I can't ever be with any one of them again. I'm not cut out to be a husband.*

He was so wrapped up in a certain idea of freedom, that it was the idea alone that suffocated him, rather than Paloma herself or anything she did or didn't do.

On top of that, her unearned advantages had begun to eat at him. Paloma, beacon of rich, white privilege. She was self-conscious about it, apologetic. *What would you do?* She asked him, *if you had been born with the same advantages? Give them up? What about your own white privilege?*

Paloma had Celine, a loving father, all the wealth in the world, was beautiful, educated, had every chance to succeed; he had a mum with a drug problem and scattered parenting abilities, no money, and a dad who never cared enough to even see him born let alone stick around after that. Everything he had — and he was getting more every day — he had worked hard for. If he hadn't worked so hard, who knows what he'd be. It wasn't Paloma's fault, he knew, logically; but seeing her house, her ease with everything and everyone in the world, seeing how she never gave money or success a second thought, the way she just assumed abundance, it soured him. It was a reminder that life was unfair. He wasn't proud of those thoughts. Did it change anything? Did he have the emotional scope to move past those same conflicts now?

If being with someone were only about love, how much easier would the world be? Being an adult meant understanding that love didn't conquer all; it was a realisation that George resented, even if he had resigned himself to it. He wanted to love her, to prove he could be better.

This thought was far from comforting. He fell asleep in the plastic hospital chair thinking it, anyway.

—

It took a confused hot moment for him to realise the incessant buzzing was coming from outside his head.

His phone vibrated in the near dark and he answered an unknown number blearily, 'George Green, fucking idiot.'

'Mr Green? It's Sergeant Lewis. I've been trying to reach you.'

'I'm sorry, there have been some personal matters, the cyclone . . .'

'Are you on the island?'

'No I'm in hospital on the mainland.'

'Everything okay?'

'No, my . . . Paloma Knightley has been seriously injured. She's unconscious. A blow to the head.'

Lewis paused for a moment. 'I'm not far off myself. I'll come in. Be there soon.'

———

Outside in the hushed hospital hallway George felt time was geologic. After about a billion years, Sergeant Lewis arrived, quiet and determined.

'We've come into some new information,' she said. 'I wanted to discuss it with you.'

'Okay.'

'It concerns Walter Eveleigh. He's been renting an apartment under an assumed name here on the mainland. We've conducted a search and found, among other things, a laptop which was reported as stolen from the Knightley family home. I think it's time we pool our resources, don't you think?'

He did think. It took some convincing to get him away from Paloma's bedside, but the lure of finally resolving this mess finally got him moving, and he went down to the station with Lewis.

—

Police stations were all alike. George was wired on the fluorescent lights, instant coffee, worry, anger, and needed to get back to Paloma's side more than anything he'd ever wanted.

He was keen to call the forensics team and find out their news — so they decided to do it together. He shared everything new he had with the police. Then they were ready to contact the Sydney team.

George sat with Lewis in an office the colour of sour milk.

After jumps and false starts, they had a connection with the lead investigator in Sydney, a man named Andy.

'We've been trying to reach you up there,' Andy said. 'Looks like we've got something.

'We probably wouldn't have found a thing, given the scope of operations, if it weren't for those three names you supplied, George. They led us in the right direction. And it turns out that they were connected to what appears to be a significant fraud operation within the company.'

'Who?' George asked, knowing the answer.

'Walter Eveleigh. We're still uncovering the scope, but it looks like he has been embezzling from the company for some time. I've got to stress that these types of crimes are hard to investigate and hard to prosecute. We need more concrete evidence.'

'So those three names, they're the key evidence. Do you know how she came across them?' asked Lewis.

'Slipped under her door,' George replied.

'However they were found,' said Andy, 'turns out they're ghosts and zombies.'

George looked at Andy on the screen for a long moment, wondering if he'd finally lost it. Or Andy had. Or both.

'Ghost employees,' Andy continued. 'When a person's on a payroll system, who either doesn't exist at all, a ghost; or if they're an actual person who once worked for the company and doesn't any longer, a zombie.'

So the letter had been right all along. It could be that Adam had been setting Walt up; it was more likely he had tried to blackmail Walt and failed.

Something else was echoing in George's mind: *a hard blow to the head*.

'Two of the names were zombies,' continued Andy. 'Working travellers who had been employed as casuals on the island years ago. The third was a ghost, fictional. So that led us to an extensive — and I'm talking more than seven years and ten million dollars and counting — network of zombies and ghosts.

'With so many employees, spread across here and Sydney, the high turnover rate of the industry, as well as a centralised HR, it's not a surprise that no one picked anything up. We're still looking into potential accomplices. There was no need to even hide the payments. From the surface, it all looks like normal transactions. Once the ghost has been generated in the system, it's pretty much automated.

'The zombie staff were simply never terminated. The system was tweaked so no timesheets were needed, and they were location non-specific, so performance reviews and so on were never generated, plus the fraud employees were all on salary.

'Some of the ghosts were on staff for years, others were created and retired regularly, matching casual staff movements. The thing about ghosts is it's almost impossible to find them without a tip-off. Without Paloma's names, even if we had been looking, we likely never would have detected anything. When we knew what to look for — names with little personnel information, no physical location specified, PO boxes or the same mailing address, and ultimately, payments that went into the same bank account. That's not taking into consideration any that were paid in cash, which is also possible.

'All we needed to do was investigate who was receiving the payments. If they were cash, then the trail would go cold — and perhaps some were. Thankfully the system, like most these days, mostly used direct deposit. So a bank account was needed; after that it was just a matter of time. We found that the account was under what ultimately was a false name, and it seems Adam helped to provide false identification documents needed for the latest account — because the account was changed several times.

'As the person in charge of HR and personnel on the island itself, and the ultimate authorisation of payroll, Walter Eveleigh had both access and opportunity.'

'Enough to proceed with prosecution?' asked Lewis.

'Not yet. Give us time.'

'Great work,' said Lewis. 'We'll be in touch.' She closed the laptop.

'Which us leads us to the question,' she said, 'if Walter — and Adam — are behind the fraud, and Adam was looking to point the finger at his boss, who has the strongest motive for killing Adam?'

'And who would want Paloma out of the way if she was on their trail?' George said.

'Or you.' Lewis said.

'What about this staged robbery, the stuff found in Walt's apartment here?'

'We're still going through the computer. It hasn't been wiped. We don't know what to look for.'

'Do you think I could take a look?'

'I don't know if that's the best idea.'

'I know the case,' George continued. 'And it's thanks to the forensics team I organised in Sydney that you found what you have on the fraud, which is the best possible lead in Adam's murder.'

She looked at him for a moment. 'Well, no promises. I'll see what I can do. In the meantime, you stay here on the mainland. Get some sleep. Be there when Paloma wakes up.'

'I'm pretty beat.' He agreed.

'No shit,' she said, not unkindly.

—

Back at the hospital, George checked on Paloma, then finally fell into a deep and soundless sleep on a lumpy sofa.

When he woke he checked in on her again — no change — and went back to the station to see if there was any progress to him viewing the laptop.

He brought Lewis good coffee. She waved him in.

They'd cracked access easy enough, but the laptop was old and clogged with the digital detritus of a life. Old Mate's life. George clicked and clicked, folder after folder. It was almost exclusively work related. Saved emails, records, files. Old Mate was systematic about it, and George's eyes blurred after spending hours at the screen.

But then. *Walter.doc.* George opened what appeared to be a contract. George read:

> I, Walter Eveleigh, hereby rescind any and all claims to any other position at Songbird Island Pty Ltd, apart from my current role as General Manager, Songbird Enterprises.
>
> I will not at any time take on any other role at the company, nor seek to increase my salary or bonuses under any circumstances unless approved direct by Thomas Knightley.
>
> I agree to these conditions in perpetuity, under condition that Thomas Knightley's solicitor will release agreed-upon information publicly.
>
> Signed: Walter Eveleigh, 1/12/95
> Signed: Thomas Knightley 1/12/95

What was going on? Why had Walt given up any career advancement and income increase? What did Old Mate have on him, and why had he kept it quiet from Celine? And what did the lawyer have on Walt?

George's thoughts raced.

He continued his search. There was something else odd in Old Mate's banking statements. A recurring payment, each month, to the same account, for $4000. It went back as far as George could scroll. Then, just before his death, two transfers of $500,000 apiece. To a Dora Williams. Where had he heard that name before? George jotted down the name and bank account number to look into later.

——

Once he was done with the computer, George felt he had to get out of there, fast. He couldn't wait around while the investigation raked through company's financial records, sitting there, doing nothing. Not when it looked like Walt could be the one who hurt Paloma, who could be Adam's killer.

He wanted to fight the whole world. It was a feeling that manifested as fighting its representative: a single man.

14.

After the ravages of the storm the island presented a new face. No longer swept, kept pristine, now branches and debris lay everywhere, a confused mess choking the small roads, clogging up the beaches. The palm trees stripped of all their leaves. Even the sky looked disordered and forlorn.

The sea was skimmed tenderly with needlepoints of light. Yachts were tipped drunkenly on their sides, their masts almost horizontal, one beached. *Chakra* was one of a few that seemed mostly intact. Part of the roof of the main hotel was peeled open like a can. Glass shards glinted in the light. Staff in bright T-shirts and thongs quietly picked through the rubbish, clearing branches, looking confused. The air of disaster had started to fade and reality needed to be dealt with.

He knew how they felt.

George went back to the house. Iris was red-eyed on a sofa, looking dazed.

'How are you holding up?' he asked.

'It's too much, I didn't want all this,' she said quietly. 'Adam, and now Paloma's in hospital. Any news?'

'She's still unconscious,' George said.

'How did it happen?' she asked in a wild whisper.

'The doctor says a blunt blow to the head. Something must've come loose in the storm, hit her head. She's lucky, they say.'

'Yes,' Iris said, looking worried. 'Please be careful, it's —'

Walter's voice sliced the air.

'You're back,' he said.

Iris shrank, and then left.

'Just picking up a few things for Paloma. I'll be heading over to the mainland on the afternoon ferry.'

'How is she?'

'Still unconscious.'

'You've seen the police?' said Walt. 'Any leads on Adam?'

'They aren't telling me anything about it,' he said.

'Who do you think did it?'

'I wouldn't like to say.'

'Isn't it your job to say?'

'It's with the police now. I'm not here to investigate anything anymore. I'm just here for Paloma.'

'Of course you are. But the suspect pool's pretty shallow, isn't it? Who had motive, means, opportunity?'

'Whoever it was, I'm sure the police will find the culprit.'

'I'm sure they will,' Walt replied. 'Anyway I'll leave you to it. Lots to do. Still pretty crazy around here.'

George watched Walt leave, as he walked down the front path and towards the main hotel. When he was sure he was out of sight, George flitted fast up the stairs into Walt's office.

—

Picking locks was part of the PI's tradecraft. It just so happened that George enjoyed it, too. The orderliness of them. The satisfying sound they made when they opened. The delicacy of picking without leaving a trace. It was like learning a new language every time. He spoke to Walt's desk drawer lock, with his makeshift tools, gleaned from the kitchen and island's tool supply.

It took a while. He was patient.

Inside he saw a little book filled with numbers and dates, snapped photos on his phone of a few of its pages.

He re-locked the drawer, and left, making sure no one was around before heading up to Celine and Walt's bedroom.

In the bedroom, he found the gun — Tom's old one — where he had expected, hidden behind the bedside just as it was before. Now he unloaded it, pocketing the bullets, before putting it carefully back in place.

—

What would she want? She loved fancy pyjamas. George felt less comfortable flitting through Paloma's top drawer than picking a lock as he had moments ago, he found pyjamas, underwear, a couple of T-shirts, leggings, her hairbrush, and a randomly selected bottle from her baffling array of skincare, which he stuffed into a bag. The room was full of her smell.

'C'mon, you fucken idiot,' he said to himself under his breath, and closed the door behind him.

———

The path down to the beach was still strewn with leaves, branches, and unidentifiable pieces of things-that-had-been. He padded down as if he were on his way for an afternoon dip, but his heart was beating hard. If he knew what he was doing, and he wasn't at all sure that he did, then this would be a turning point. Perhaps, after all, it was nothing. *Tell my lungs that*, he thought, rasping.

Palm Beach was a perfectly formed stretch of silica sand, curving gently in a protected cove, ideal for kids and water-sports, kayaks and canoes and morning yoga classes. Its picture-perfect lustre was dimmed, now, in the grey after-wash of the cyclone, surfaces marred by the upheaval. No one was there. The tourists had all gone, to tell their stories of *My honeymoon paradise turned nightmare*, and the resort would close for months, haemorrhaging money while it underwent repairs.

The staff were back on the main street, in the hotel and bungalows, tidying up as best they could. But who knew when it would be back to what it was. How long it would take for tourists to trust this place again. George walked down the stretch of sand to a secluded point at the far tip of the beach, hoping like hell that he was right and that Walt was taking his bait. If there was going to be a confrontation, he could at least draw Walt away from everyone else, so only George himself was in any danger. He waited.

It began to rain. At first softly, it soon gained momentum, a needling shower blowing in gusts in the wind. As he began to walk against it, he saw a figure in the distance, and his heart raced against his ribs. *This is it*.

As George approached, the blurred figure took the shape of a person: Walt. Walt's right hand: extended, holding a gun loosely.

'Walt,' George said over the rain.

'You don't seem very surprised to see me,' he said.

'What's with the gun?' George replied.

'I'm going to shoot you with it,' he said. 'Not that I want to. It can't be helped now.'

'Why's that?'

'I know you know. If you are any good at your job — and I have reason to think you are — you've worked at least some of it out. Enough to incriminate me, certainly.'

'That you killed Adam?'

'Did you ever find out his real name?' Walt asked. 'Did you put that together?'

'Chris Mosely.' He replied.

'Try again! No ideas? Well you might like to ask our houseguest, the charming and delightful Mrs Iris Quade. Not using her married name anymore, but I think you see my point.'

Quade. Quade. Where had he . . . oh damn.

'It's funny watching people's brains work. I can see that single neuron firing, and there it is, it's clicking into place isn't it? Iris's husband didn't go missing, she knew exactly where he was and what he was doing, here on the island, pretending to be someone called Adam.'

'But why?'

'The usual. Money. Adam was blackmailing Celine, Iris was *attempting* to blackmail me, and between them they were trying to take me, and the company for that matter, for all we're worth.'

'But you put a stop to it.'

'Someone had to. After all my years of hard work, I wasn't going to let them walk in and just take what I'd earned. Again.'

'What you'd taken, you mean?'

'Provoking a man with the gun? That's an interesting life choice. You're good at making bad choices, aren't you?

'I only took what was rightfully mine. What Old Mate made sure I'd never get my hands on. He took care of Celine and Paloma, I'll give him that. But I was the one working my youth away for him. Celine and Paloma couldn't care less about the business. Do you think they deserve all that money? Do you think they even like having it? I suppose you have a fair idea of what Paloma likes.

'There are enough entitled people in the world, and those two haven't faced the real world, the one we know about, their whole lives. It wouldn't hurt them to have a glimpse of reality. Old Mate shielded them from it. I think they'll grow because of it. Celine certainly will. No. You work, you receive. And I was the one who earned it,' he continued, lowering his gun, sharply eyed by George.

'But Old Mate had something on you. Made sure you wouldn't progress. What was it?'

'Tom had issues of his own. Thought it better to sweep things under rugs than let them hurt his girls.'

'An affair? Is that was he had?'

'It doesn't matter now.'

'Adam found out about the embezzling, didn't he?'

'I brought him into it. A mistake. And naturally he decided to up stakes. His pocket money from Celine wasn't enough, which he stupidly thought I didn't know about, and I wasn't giving Iris a single dollar, so he decided to try and extort me. That was his big mistake. He should have known what kind of man I was, after the attempted blackmail with Iris. I'm not the sort to budge.'

'So you killed him.'

'He got killed attempting to drug and kidnap my wife, let me remind you. The world's a better place without him.'

'And me? Is the world a better place without me?'

'You seem like a good enough guy. But I'm in a corner now. Can't be helped.'

'And the police? They know as much as I do.'

'I don't think so, mate.'

Walt pointed the dark shape of his gun towards George again. The rain still came in windy gusts, pounding them indiscriminately. Everything on the beach was indistinct, blurs of grey and beige. George had unconsciously stepped backwards, inching away as Walt spoke, and was ankle deep in water.

'Walt! Stop!' They heard Iris's scream through the sweeping wind.

'Iris, no! What are you doing?' yelled George.

'Stay out of this. Go back home, Iris, I'm warning you.'

'And let you shoot someone else too? It's not going to end this way.'

'How's it going to end?' said Walt, turning to point the gun towards her. 'With you saving the day? Me paying you off? Or maybe with me leaving Celine for you? Is that what's going on in your head?' he laughed. 'You're more deluded than your husband was.'

She laughed back mirthlessly. 'Your ego really is astonishing.'

George tried to deflect Walt's attention.

'Iris it's okay, do what Walt says. You don't need to get involved.'

'No one needed to get hurt,' she said wildly. 'But you killed him! Why did you do it?'

'Adam? I mean Andrew? Or is it Chris? It's hard to keep up. You know that was necessary,' Walt said. 'He was nothing but an amateur, looking to take advantage of us. He brought that upon himself and you know it. You're the only person in the world who will miss him.'

George crept up as quietly as he could behind Walt, each step feeling like it took an aeon.

Iris's eyes darted to George, and Walt swung around. Good.

'No,' he said quickly, gun on George, and as Iris leaped on him, he pulled the trigger. It went off with a shocking retort.

It took them both a moment to realise what had happened.

Walt had known the gun was empty. He had re-loaded. George thanked the universe that the shot had missed, and reached to grab the loaded gun from Walt, failed. In a storm of fists and water, George could hear Iris's screams and feel the thump of Walt's hands, arms, legs, nails, bones, skin, against his own body. George fought back as best he could, slipping in the sand into the water.

Once down, Walt tried to hold George's head under the waves, and he breathed in seawater. George was used to a little seawater, but Walt's arms were as unyielding as a cliff face. George snorted water into his nose, struggling and thinking clearly: *So this is how I die. I always knew the sea would get me. I just didn't know it would be like this.*

There was another shot and George felt a sudden release. Walt was no longer above him. George coughed up water then breathed deep, and through the mist saw Iris standing above him, shaking. Her sleeve blooming with red.

'He shot me,' she said, matter of fact.

Walter was fleeing down the beach, his figure blurred by the rain, then gone. His gun in the sea. George grabbed it, wondered if he should chase after

Walt, but his chest was raw and he was finding it hard to breathe.

'C'mon, let's go!' George said with effort. Iris grasped onto him, helping him walk, and they went up the beach and up to the main hotel.

Bloody, drenched, and with a gun in his pocket, George knew how they looked to the hotel manager.

'Get the police on the phone, DI Lewis,' he said, having lost his own phone somewhere on the beach.

'Lewis,' the voice answered.

'George Green. I'm on Songbird. Walter Eveleigh has just attempted to shoot me and has shot Iris, she's okay but needs medical attention. He's on the loose.'

Lewis took it calmly, without reprimanding George for going back, and quickly told them to stay in the hotel, call the medic, call security, and wait until the police arrived.

The manager put Iris and George in the staff sick room, a tiny space with a single bed and basic medical supplies. George washed and bandaged her arm. Iris washed and patched George's cut face with trembling hands.

'Thank you for saving my life,' he said.

At the mainland hospital, the ER waiting room was cramped and had the feeling of desperation common to all hospital emergency departments. At reception, Iris said calmly 'I've been shot. He's maybe broken a rib,' and the nurse had ushered them through immediately with a raised eyebrow.

The doctor was efficient as she took George's vitals and pressed his tender side, making George wince. An X-ray confirmed a broken rib. He was given a script for painkillers, an ice pack and orders to take it easy.

Though every inhalation reminded George of his injury, he had complete faith in recovery. Yeah, he was no longer twenty, or even thirty, but he was still steady. Not yet on the decline.

The last time he had been badly hurt he had broken a leg. Not long after Paloma had left. He'd been drunk, high, at a house party where he'd forgotten which woman he'd shown up with. Jumped off the roof into the pool. With inevitable results. That he hadn't even done it on some outrageously risky act of surfing was to his shame.

Most had thought it would spell the end of his career, contracts and endorsements. He'd surfed as soon as he could get back on a board and some ways he was better than before: meaner, with more to prove. But he was bored. So he left surfing for good, after proving he was still at his peak. He didn't tell anyone. He just didn't show up. It was sudden and total. He abandoned his manager financially as well as personally. He decided none of it mattered that much anymore.

The police were on Songbird, looking for Walt. Part of George wanted to be out looking for him too, instead of at the hospital where he knew he'd have to talk to Celine. But Paloma was there, so he stayed.

When he returned to the waiting room Iris was sitting still, looking smaller, her shoulders crumpled and her arm held tenderly to her chest. 'A graze,' she said with a weak smile. 'They say I'm lucky . . . Just my kind of luck, I suppose I'm going to need to talk to the police.'

'Yeah. Can I ask why you did it? Blackmailed your own family?'

'They have more money than they know what to do with, George. Trust me, they could afford to lose some. My family never had that much. Walt has been a bad apple since day one. I'm sad for Celine of course but it's better in some ways that she knows the kind of man she married. They're all better off without him. That the truth has come out. The rest I'm sorry about though. You won't believe me but I really am.'

'I'm sorry about your husband.'

'So am I. We had more than our share of problems. He wasn't very good for me, not that it really mattered. I still miss him.'

They sat under the fluorescent lights.

'Let's go see Paloma and Celine, though I don't suppose they will want anything to do with me after they know all of this,' she said, standing, reaching out for his hand.

George took it.

—

Celine was outside in the corridor when they approached Paloma's room, in a ward now.

'What happened to you two?' she asked, taking in George's changed gait, cut face, Iris's wrapped arm.

George exchanged looks with Iris. He'd better tell it straight.

'I'm going to see the patient,' Iris said quickly, 'the other patient,' and disappeared into the room.

'What's the story?' asked Celine.

'Broken rib. Few cuts. Celine —'

'What happened?'

'Let's go somewhere more private,' he suggested. She shrugged, looking bemused, and followed him into a waiting room that smelled like overripe bananas and antiseptic. There was a picture of a dolphin diving out of the water, three upholstered chairs, a water cooler.

'I'm sorry,' he said.

Now they were there he found that he wanted to delay telling her that her husband was violent, deceitful, a murderer, for as long as he could. But that wouldn't help anyone. He wondered, not for the first time, how much of this would be news to her anyway. How well did wives know husbands? How much did some spouses wilfully ignore what was going on? Or even get a thrill from it? If Walt wasn't above board, maybe she was into that. Whatever the case, he struggled to believe she'd known about the killing, though he knew it was possible she'd seen him that night.

'It's Walter,' he said.

'Is he okay?' she asked quickly.

'He's not hurt. The police are looking for him.'

'What on Earth for?' she said, but somewhere

in her eyes George could see that she had seen this coming. Or at least wasn't entirely surprised.

'He's under investigation. For embezzlement.'

'Embezzlement?' she echoed, cautiously.

'He's also the main suspect in Adam's murder.'

'That's ridiculous,' she said. 'I'm going home right now, we're going to sort this out.'

'Wait. I know you don't want to hear this. He is the one who did this to Iris and me, he attempted to shoot me because I found out about Adam, about the fraud.'

'I'm leaving right now. You have no idea what you're talking about.' She hissed, and whipped out of the room.

George looked at the poster, feeling drained and dirty and about half the man he used to be. If that. 'What are you so smug about?' He asked the dolphin.

179

15.

Paloma had the feeling of floating in a fast-moving current of water. Every sound was muffled and twice-removed. Covered in cotton wool. A glowing light seemed like it could be the sun, warming her watery limbs and infusing her bones. Her breath sank like vespers. Her bones were by chance and only temporarily covered with muscle and flesh.

When her mind leaped up for air, her head stung with a sudden pain, and she retreated again.

She saw that the glow was not the sun, after all, it was a light above her, in a hospital room, small and too bright, in a world full of sorrows. In that moment she didn't really mind the idea of death, because the lies, the lies which didn't help her one bit, were much better than the truth.

But then there were other words: *yes we're all going to die. But we should live anyway.*

She tried to retreat back, but the hospital light was all she could think of.

'Paloma,'

She'd rather think of the sea, open and warm —

'Paloma, please.'

'Please wake up,'

'Can you hear me?'

Paloma reached out for the light, the voice: fingers full of air. The cold ping of machines. Dry oxygen. She was warm, swathed in crisp sheets.

'Paloma?'

'What?' It sounded so full, cloudlike, rolling off her tongue like cumulus.

'How are you feeling?' the voice replied, strange to her. She opened her eyes a slit to see a mouth like a rosebud and hair an auburn cosmos.

'Lousy,' she said. 'How are you? Who are you?'

Where was Cee? George? Her mind stayed awake to get another glimpse.

'Pal,' George's voice. George's hand holding hers.

'You never call me Pal,' she said, a tight throat. 'It must be bad. Where am I?'

'She doesn't remember?' Iris's voice, quieter.

'She's going to be hazy for a bit, that's completely normal. You've been in an accident, you're in hospital,' the unknown voice said, louder.

'I'm okay,' she said.

'It could have been a lot worse. It's just your good luck George was there to help you.'

'What happened?' Paloma could feel her cells being pulled back into reality, and as they did so, every single one of them hurt.

'Blow to the head. In the storm.'

'You'll be all right after some rest. Take it easy,' said the doctor.

'I'm not very good at taking it easy,' she replied sleepily.

'The button's here if you need a nurse,' the doctor said, and either went invisible, or left.

'Do you need anything?' asked Iris.

'A whiskey sour.'

'A juice will have to do. Can she drink? I saw a vending machine down the hall,' Iris said, and disappeared.

'Where's Cee? Jude?' Paloma asked, then fell back asleep.

———

The weird twilight of the hospital was disorienting, or maybe it was the morphine. Paloma didn't know if it was night or day when she woke periodically, nothing to link her to time except the sound of the machines, and the visit of a nurse or doctor on their rounds.

As the dosage of the drugs decreased, the lines and light began to clear, bouncing back into recognisable shapes.

'How long have I been here?' she asked George, who always seemed to be next to her, sometimes on his laptop.

'Two days. I think they're going to let you leave soon,' he said.

'Home,' she said. She wanted to be home more than anything. 'Where's Cee?'

'She's at home with Jude. They'll be here soon.'

'Paloma,' George asked, 'do you know the name Dora Williams?'

'Of course,' she said with a hazy smile. 'That's Mum.' She drifted back off into a kind of sleep.

—

Paloma didn't see her sister until the day of her release from hospital. Celine came, and they hugged for a long time, each thinking: *She looks so tired.*

'Are you okay?'

'I'm the one who should be asking that,' Celine said.

'I've got the all clear. I just need to take it easy for a bit. I'm lucky you and George were there.'

They hugged again, this time Paloma felt Celine cry.

'What's wrong? I'm okay, really.'

'I don't want to worry you. You've already been through all this,' she said.

'Cee, what's wrong?'

'It's Walt,' she said. 'The police are looking for him, I don't know where he is. They're saying he's been stealing from the company, can you believe that? That he was involved in Adam's death.'

Paloma didn't know how to begin answering that, so she didn't. She just hugged Celine and leant on her as they left the hospital to go back home.

—

The waves were dark. Paloma and George were sitting on the deck of the ferry going back to Songbird Island and the sea felt mountainous, Paloma's stomach lurching as it dipped and rose. She was sitting next to an emergency orange life ring, wondering if she should have stayed at the hospital after all. She stared at her shoes most of the way, trying to regain equilibrium.

'You alright?' George had left Iris inside where she was flirting with a day-tripper on the grimy plastic seats. Celine was reading next to Iris.

'No, I'm not okay,' Paloma said.

'Oh my God, what's wrong?' he said, panicked.

'No, I mean I'm okay — it doesn't hurt too much or anything, I feel like myself again. I'm just thinking about my life. It's not really okay anymore, is it?'

After a long pause he said, 'I think you and I should get back together.'

'George —' she said.

'I know, I've got no right. I'm asking anyway. I can't do anything else but love you.'

But he didn't understand.

'I can't be hurt anymore,' Paloma said. 'My heart can't handle it.'

'I say love, you say hurt? I don't want to hurt you, and I won't.'

'You can't promise that. No one can. Loving me isn't the same thing as being with me. I love you. But I can't be with you.'

It was clearly not the reaction he was hoping for.

'Things change,' Paloma said. 'I want the whole thing: marriage, kids, wild romantic love, boring house chores. I don't want someone who wants me when he's feeling vulnerable or lost, someone who doesn't really want to commit to me. I know what I need now.'

'You think I don't want that?'

'Do you?'

'I've never wanted anything as much.'

'But for how long? Until your rib is better? Until there's a wave you can't miss? Until you decide that you've changed your mind? I don't know that you can be honest with yourself, let alone with me.'

'I've changed. I'm trying to change.'

'I don't want change. I want stability.'

—

At home, Paloma wanted a bed, hot tea, painkillers, about three weeks of sleep. She got the first three.

16.

He normally didn't buy into the regret scenario, but now he'd make an exception. After Paloma had told him she wasn't interested on the ferry, George had walked down to the beach, puked, and sat on the sand feeling sorry for himself. He knew he was about to make things even worse. He wanted to protect her. But now he was breaking everything right open, telling her that her life was a lie.

If he'd never come to the island, never met her, or any of her family, things would be okay. Even that was a lie and he knew it.

The last few weeks left him full of regret but he knew he'd never regret the time he spent with Paloma, despite the fact it'd ended because of him. It happened. It was beautiful. And it was over. His rib bit into his lungs. He'd pack up his bag, go back to Sydney, sit on the couch, drink, marathon the *X-Files*, and everything would be right with the world again.

But how could he leave Paloma, or even Celine, with Walt still at large? Whether Paloma wanted him or not didn't matter. The police were stationed at the house, and he knew he couldn't leave knowing that

Walt could come back at any time. He knew Paloma and Celine would want to know. He knew the truth was the right thing. Just look at the chaos that lies and secrets had made here.

I'm fucked, he said to himself, with resignation. What did you do even when you knew you were going to lose? You went forward anyway.

'Paloma, Celine.'

'Dad used to call us like that,' Paloma said idly. 'Like it was all one word. *Palomaceline.*'

'What?' Celine said bluntly, tired. She'd lost patience with everyone except Jude. George most of all: the bearer of bad tidings.

'I have some news. It's hard for me to say, so I'm just going to say it.'

'Jesus, George, what?' asked Paloma.

'When I was looking through your dad's personal finances I came across an ongoing payment each month, not huge but not insubstantial, regular and longstanding. It was to someone in particular. The name on the account was Dora Williams.'

They looked at him, Paloma confused, Celine's anger flashing.

'What the hell does that mean? Why was he paying someone using mum's name?'

'He was paying your mum.'

They were both silent.

'What do you mean?' said Paloma.

'Our mum is dead,' said Celine.

'No. She isn't. She's alive and living in Tasmania.' He spoke as softly as he could.

'That's insane. Why would dad lie to us? Where has she been all these years?'

How could he tell Paloma, or even Celine, that their beloved dad had not only known that their mum was still alive, but was paying her money every month to stay out of their lives, to stay as quiet as the dead? What was the going price on that? $4K a month and a million for the rest of her life?

'I think it's best if she tells you that.'

He pushed a piece of paper with a phone number written on it across the table.

—

Iris was assisting the police in their investigation. She seemed happy to, and George didn't ask what charges would be made against her, or what deal she'd made.

'We need to know what's going on,' Paloma said to George. 'What's really going on. Cee needs to know everything. We need to clear the air, and you should do it.'

She was right. He'd asked Iris, Celine, Paloma and Jude to gather at the big table, under Old Mate's watchful gaze, and George spoke, for the last time, before leaving for Sydney.

'I want to share with you everything I've learned while I've investigated this case,' he said, and looked around the room. Iris, uncomfortable and red-eyed,

Cee cool and angry, Paloma like a warm beating heart, Jude silently buzzing with energy.

'Paloma received an anonymous letter and asked me to come here to look into it. It was delivered by hand on Songbird, so it had to be from someone who had either visited recently or was based here. The letter claimed that Walt was embezzling funds from Songbird Island Limited, and had been doing so for some time. It also made several other claims of a more personal nature.

'The letter said Walt had been conducting extra-marital affairs. Which only convinced me further that whoever wrote the letter had a personal motive. Letters of this kind often have personal grudges behind them.

'I was right. The letter was driven by personal motives. Adam, we found out, was in fact an alias,' he hesitated, looking at Iris. She smiled sadly. Nodded.

'His real name is Andrew Quade and he has form, mostly white-collar crime. He was married for the last five years to Iris.'

'Wait,' Celine said. 'That's ridiculous, I've seen photos of your husband . . .'

'Dyed his hair, shaved his beard,' Iris said. 'And you'd never actually met him in real life, so we figured you'd never suspect.'

'Never suspect what exactly?' Celine said.

'Iris and Andrew had a con,' continued George. 'They'd come up here under the guise of a tragedy, swindle Walt, and then flee together, cashed up and none of you — except Walt — any the wiser.'

'Is this true, Iris?' Celine asked.

'I'm sorry, I really am Celine. It was his idea. We were broke, in debt. And you all have so much money. More than you can ever need, and Walt is bad news.'

'Adam was first to come up here for the EA role, and once he was here he didn't like what he found. He began to hate Walt. Who knows why. Maybe he was jealous of the man's success. He was good at ingratiating himself, and he soon got on Walt's good side. With a little digging, and maybe a few confidences from Walt, Adam soon recognised a fellow con man. Iris followed after some time had passed, began an affair with Walt, and then Adam wrote the first letter to Paloma.'

George cast a quick look at Celine. She was watching the table intently.

'Adam not only wanted money, he wanted to cause as much trouble as possible, so he wrote the letter incriminating Walt. He also attempted to blackmail Celine, and possibly humiliate Walt even more, with a video supposedly showing Celine and Adam in an adulterous affair.'

'As I investigated the case, I had forensic accountants look into Songbird Island's finances and the claims against Walt. Embezzlement is surprisingly difficult to uncover, especially when it has been done well, and even harder to prove in a way that adds up to a conviction. We probably wouldn't have come up with anything provable, had it not been for yet another anonymous tip-off Paloma received, a piece of paper containing three names, which was slipped under Paloma's door here in the house. Likely by Adam again, or possibly Iris.'

'Phoebe Harris. Gregg Coleman. Sean Longworth. It seemed someone was deliberately leading us down a certain path, and we weren't moving quickly enough. It was only when we looked into these names, that the truth became clear.

'Someone had been creating fake employees. A complicated scheme. So the team traced as many as they could over the last ten years, looking at where their annual income was paid into. The cumulative loss is . . . already very significant.

'Then there was the so-called break-in. Complete lie from start to finish. Walt knew who I was, knew I was getting closer, and staged a break-in, in which the laptop and several other trifles were taken to make it seem opportunistic. And he added a further red herring by wearing Celine's kimono as he did so.'

'Why would Walt steal anything?' said Celine. 'It's all crazy, he had everything. He never even asked for a raise!'

'Very few embezzlers know the word "enough". Walt was also party to a certain contract that Tom made him sign years ago, that ultimately meant he could not progress in his career at Songbird, or financially benefit from the family fortune.'

'Have you lost it?' said Celine.

'How much money are we talking?' said Paloma.

'At least $10 million has been embezzled that we can track so far. I'm not finished,' he said. 'Unfortunately.'

'I think you've said enough,' said Celine, eyes flashing.

'I was becoming a problem. And so was Paloma.

After getting rid of Adam, Walt found that he still hadn't sorted it all out. I was investigating, and now his sister-in-law was too. Giving me access to business information, helping me set up the forensics investigation with the CEO in Sydney, following Iris, asking questions. He wanted me and Paloma gone. He almost succeeded that day with Paloma.'

'You're saying he tried . . . Walt . . . to kill me?' said Paloma, paling.

'It wasn't an accident. Someone hit your head that day. Someone who thought it would be easier if you just vanished.'

'Dad wouldn't do that,' Jude said, and Celine clutched his hand, which looked giant in her own.

'You're a crackpot,' said Celine. 'Taking money is one thing. I don't know how you could even suggest he'd hurt Paloma.'

'I didn't investigate the scene after it happened, I wouldn't have thought there was a scene to investigate . . . an accident in the cyclone, everyone thought. But there were people there that day. Iris saw Walt approach Paloma, and she was the one who suggested to myself and the police that maybe it wasn't as accidental as it appeared.'

'Iris?' said Celine. 'Because she's so trustworthy?' She stood, really angry now, 'Are you quite done?' she asked George. 'Now that my entire life is completely ruined? Now that you've said all this about Walt in front of our son? Have you done enough?'

'I'm sorry.' said Iris. 'But you're better off knowing exactly what kind of man he is.'

'Tell yourself that if it helps,' said Celine. 'Leave my house.'

'So, where's Dad?' Jude asked.

'The police are looking for him now,' George replied, and though it hurt like hell, he didn't look away from the boy's pained eyes.

'I'm sorry.'

Epilogue

The police found Walt hiding out on *Chakra*, living off of warm Champagne and the remains of the well-stocked pantry. Celine and Jude had raced to the marina when they heard, in time to see Walt, hand-cuffed, being taken to the water police vessel. George and Paloma followed behind. Jude motioned to go to his dad, already breathless; but Celine reached out for his arm.

'We'll talk to him later, love.'

Walt looked tired even at a distance, those broad shoulders in an unfamiliar slouch, his hair in his eyes, his shirt crumpled. He didn't look up, his eyes focused on the shoes of the cop in front of him.

—

It was an unruffled day in Coogee. The sea was sleepy; the sloping street bordered with bougainvillea, pink and waxy green, bursting over a rickety wooden fence.

Paloma was barefoot, walking. It was a sort of peace: Paloma, in a street that had grown familiar, the spill of colour in the sedate day — the calm in her eyes too.

Peace. It meant many things. To Paloma, mostly this: someone to love, someone to love her back, a home, something to look forward to, being busy enough to give the day structure and meaning. All these things she had. Is that enough? Enough for happiness? Paloma didn't know. Peace, after everything that'd happened, was enough.

She stepped into a drowsy café, sat at a wooden table, her hair falling around her face, and eased into windy thoughts. She had a tea and a good book. She got a text:

meet me down the beach?

And that seemed like the best idea of all.

On the cool, near-empty beach, George lazily traced the network of small, perfectly round freckles on Paloma's back with his finger. Joining the dots of her bodily constellations, naming them:

A pear.

Twelve o'clock.

Paraguay.

'How'd it go with Dora?' He asked.

'Alright,' Paloma said. 'She's nervous about the idea of me going down there. We'll take it slow. Just get to know one another. Nothing else needs to come of it, I just want to know about her.'

They'd talked several times on the phone, and the daughters had heard the re-written past.

When George had found out about the payment to Dora back on the island, he'd dug. He had found

Dora's birth certificate, the marriage record to Tom; but there was no death certificate. Paloma and Celine just had their dad's word that she was dead, along with the undeniable fact she wasn't there. All that time, Tom had lied to his daughters. Why?

George tracked the paper records of Dora's life. She now lived in Tasmania, where she had been in and out of rehab. NA. AA. A drunk and disorderly twenty years back, no charges pressed. She was an alcoholic, a user. Supposing she'd left the family and couldn't bear the guilt, so told Old Mate to tell the girls she had died at her request; was that it? Or had Tom pressed her into leaving, thinking they were better off without her, was that why he paid her off? What would happen now he had died? Would Dora stick to the agreement? Happy with her million?

George had found her phone number. He'd been sitting in the hotel restaurant, nearly alone, the tourists all gone, skeleton crew at work. Tourists would be gone for a long time. He dialled.

'Hello?' A woman's raspy voice answered.

'Is this Dora Williams?'

'It is.'

'Dora, my name's George Green. I'm a private investigator, working on behalf of Paloma Knightley.'

There was a long silence.

'. . . Hello?'

A sigh, as if pulled from the depths of the earth.

'I was wondering if you'd find me.'

Dora had been an alcoholic when she married Tom, when she was pregnant, even after the girls had been born. Things had spiralled after Paloma had come along; Dora was getting worse. When she dropped Paloma, cutting her baby's head so she needed to have stitches, things had come to an end. The booze or her family, Old Mate had said. It was one or the other. Tom could take Dora at her worst, he loved her, but he wouldn't put his girls in danger. Dora knew she wouldn't, couldn't stop drinking, and felt consumed by the guilt of hurting her child, so she left. Old Mate thought of her as dead after that, and thought it was easier for the girls that way too. In his drive to protect them he told them the only lie he could.

Paloma and George. Warm and close. As they'd been so many times before. With unhurried sleepiness, stirring sensuality, blessed familiarity. Fat raindrops dimpling the sea, light wandering across the waves as they sat on the sand together.

There was love. There was the sea. Sometimes there was unbidden grace, and they both knew it. There was hurt too, and there were times when they had nothing to offer one another except for their own kind of light in the dark. Life was painful. Life was beautiful. The world was suffering, but not only that.

Paloma and George looked out on the sea, its flashing, white-tipped waves. The light was soft, a nest of cumulus at the horizon making outlines cottony and indistinct. Despite the low light of day it would linger, that tranquil twilight; it would be a long, long time before it was dark.

Acknowledgements

I'd like to give warm thanks to all of the brilliant colleagues, friends, and family who have helped to bring this book into being. I'm grateful for the team at Seizure and Brio Books, especially to my publisher and editor Alice Grundy, whose belief, flawless taste and insightful editing not only lifted my writing but my spirits; it was a pleasure to bring my debut novella into the world with you.

I'd like to thank my grandparents Terry and Sylvia for their love, encouragement, and book-loving DNA; and to Mum, who never got to read the final book but who I know would be proud.

I have very special thanks to give to the three M's in my life: Mat, Mel and Mia. Mel, you gave me space at your art deco house that golden summer when I first started writing this book, and endless encouragement ever since; Mia, your creative mind, joy, and sheer writing talent inspire me every day; and lastly thank you to Mat, for your incredible heart, invaluable support, and ridiculous generosity — for everything.

Viva la Novella is an annual prize awarded for short works between twenty and fifty thousand words. Since its beginnings in 2013 the award has published sixteen short novels by sixteen outstanding authors.

For more information, please visit our website
www.seizureonline.com

VIVA LA NOVELLA 2020 WINNERS
Late Sonata by Bryan Walpert
978-1-922267-23-8 (print) | 978-1-922267-24-5 (digital)
Dark Wave by Lana Guineay
978-1-922267-25-2 (print) | 978-1-922267-26-9 (digital)

VIVA LA NOVELLA 2019 WINNERS
Listurbia by Carly Cappielli
978-1-925589-87-0 (print) | 978-1-925589-88-7 (digital)
Offshore by Joshua Mostafa
978-1-925589-89-4 (print) | 978-1-925589-90-0 (digital)

VIVA LA NOVELLA 2018 WINNERS
Swim by Avi Duckor-Jones
978-1-925589-50-4 (print) | 978-1-925589-51-1 (digital)
The Bed-Making Competition by Anna Jackson
978-1-925589-52-8 (print) | 978-1-925589-53-5 (digital)